SEAL TEAM SIX:

No More

Doug Murray

A Dynamite Entertainment Book

Published by Dynamite
113 Gaither Dr., STE 205
Mount Laurel, NJ 08054

Edited by Hannah Elder
Cover design by Jason Ullmeyer

Nick Barrucci, CEO / Publisher
Juan Collado, President / COO
Joe Rybandt, Senior Editor
Brandon Dante Primavera, Director of IT / Operations
Rich Young, Director of Business Development
Hannah Elder, Associate Editor
Molly Mahan, Associate Editor
Josh Johnson, Art Director
Jason Ullmeyer, Senior Graphic Designer
Keith Davidsen, Marketing Manager
Chris Caniano, Production Assistant
Katie Hidalgo, Graphic Designer

Visit us online at www.DYNAMITE.com

Library of Congress Cataloging-in-Publication Data TK
Printed in the United States of America
Published simultaneously in Canada

ISBN: 978-1606905111   1606905112

This book is dedicated to all the men and women who have worn the uniform in the service of their country.

Prologue

Darkness surrounded Flame as he crouched with the front of his left shoulder just touching a wall of some kind, the familiar shape of an M4 cradled in his arms. *Where the hell am I?* he asked himself. *What am I supposed to do?*

He shook his head—felt a familiar weight on it. *Night vision!* He fumbled for the boxy system, and pulled it down in front of his eyes. *Now where's that switch...?*

Something clicked under his questing fingers and everything changed. *I'm in a big room of some kind.* Flame studied the green-tinged one-dimensional reality that spread around him. *Boxes and crates everywhere.* He tapped the huge crate he'd thought was a wall. *Big suckers...* He shook his head. *Supply dump, maybe...* He glanced to his front. *Looks like an access door up ahead there...*

He sensed movement somewhere behind him.

Shit! Flame turned toward the movement, clicking off the safety of his M4 with automatic precision. *Where did that come from?* He strained eyes and ears for more information—anything that might tell him what he'd gotten himself into—but all he could hear was the hammering sound of rain hitting what must have been a metal roof. Any other subtler sound was all but inaudible against *that* cacophony.

Flame stood completely still, eyes flicking from side to side, waiting for...

What?

Suddenly, he heard the familiar clatter of an AK-47 coming from somewhere behind him. Flame whirled toward the new sound, rifle barrel swiveling to bear.

There was a flicker of movement.

It came from that doorway! Flame raised the M4, aiming it at the doorjamb. *As soon as the bastard sticks his head out to try again, I'll take it off and...*

There was movement to his right as a tall, rather angular figure slid to a halt behind a large box of some kind. The figure waved to him...

Re-Pete?

The new arrival signaled to Flame that he was going to leapfrog forward and motioned for him to give covering fire.

Flame reacted automatically, stroking the trigger of his M4 to produce carefully aimed three-round bursts.

Re-Pete moved as soon as the first three rounds went downrange, moving across the floor and flattening himself alongside that enigmatic door. He gave Flame a series of signals, calling upon him to put three more rounds through the door, then hold fire and follow. Flame touched the trigger again and, as the last round whipped by him, Re-Pete swung into a crouch and prepared to move through the door.

"NO!" Flame screamed the word as a stab of something that most people would have recognized as fear suddenly stabbed through him.

There was something terribly wrong about that door!

His agonized cry cut across the constant slam of raindrops on tin, loud enough to be heard by anyone in the room—everyone except Re-Pete, whose tall figure moved fluidly through the door, waving for Flame to follow.

Flame rushed to do just that, firing blindly through that oddly familiar, somehow frightening portal. He reached the side of the door, hesitated as his hands automatically ejected the spent magazine and loaded a fresh one, a task accomplished thoughtlessly and with the precision of long practice...

I've got to go through, he told himself. *I've got to go after him!* He looked into the darkness beyond the doorway—a darkness that his night vision gear could not pierce—and froze for a long moment as he realized something. *Re-Pete is dead!* He shook his head at the realization. *He's been dead for months!* He stared into darkness. He shook his head. *Doesn't matter. He's my brother—he's expecting me to cover him...*

Flame rushed through the door—and found himself in total darkness. *What kind of place is this?* He looked around; he saw nothing, even with the enhancement of his night vision gear. *It's so dark!* He pushed the goggles up onto his forehead, strained to see something—anything—in the midnight black.

There was nothing there.

What did they teach us back in BUDS? He thought back to his last refresher course—a SEAL, after all, never stops training. The instructor's voice came to him: "In what seems total darkness, close your eyes tight—allow the pupils to dilate—then open them wide and let the light seep in at the corners..."

Flame shut his eyes tight, held them closed for an agonizingly slow ten count, then snapped them open...

And found himself in bed, staring up at a ceiling some twenty feet above him. Cold air and light filtered in from a source somewhere to his right—light that showed him that he was in a makeshift room of some kind. He could hear music booming from speakers somewhere to his left—hip-hop in an odd language.

It sounded familiar.

"Finally awake, huh?"

Flame whirled to find a petite and quite naked redhead smiling at him. "What's the matter," her grin widened. "Am I boring you?"

"Mo?" Flame reached out a trembling hand, touched the girl on the side of her face. "Is it you?"

"Don't tell me you really *are* married with rug rats!" She grabbed his hand, pulled it toward her breast. "Like your buddy told me."

"That was Manny…" Flame felt the softness of her breast under his hand, the nipple hardening under his fingers. "He was just screwing around with me …"

"As you can see, he is not here—making screwing you my job," Mo grabbed his neck, pulled him down on top of her. "Just what…" She bit his earlobe. "Are you going to do about that?"

Flame's mind whirled. Mo was dead and this place… He looked around. It was Camp Liberty—near Baghdad—he was sure of it. *But that was almost a year ago…*

He looked into Mo's sparkling eyes. *But it is her.* He ran his hand over her breasts, felt her take in a long breath, felt her shiver at his touch. *It is!* He leaned forward to kiss her…

And was interrupted by a loud klaxon.

"We're under attack!" Mo rolled out from under him, and pulled her t-shirt on. "We've got to get to a bunker!"

"Wait a minute…"

"We can't wait!" She turned earnest, worried eyes toward him. "We've got to get out of here!" She pulled her pants up, and stuck her feet, still bare, into her boots. "Come on!"

Flame reached for her—but he was too late. She rushed past him, pushing through the door just beyond the bunk.

A door that led into total darkness.

Flame cried out then—and woke as the lights came on.

"Another dream, Mr. Kelly?" The night nurse was a civilian employee of the hospital. She had taken a dislike to Flame from the day he'd arrived and made a show of noting anything he did that seemed (to her) out of the ordinary.

She was writing on his chart now—pointedly ignoring Flame as she did so.

Flame ignored her right back as he pulled on the sweat suit that he'd thrown onto the chair next to his bed. He wasn't going to get back to sleep now—might as well run for a bit.

The nurse returned his chart to its assigned place just as Flame finished lacing up his cross-trainers. "Don't forget your helmet, Mr. Kelly."

"I wouldn't think of it." Flame had started to run almost as soon as he'd been allowed to walk. At first he'd just trotted up and down the hospital corridors, exhausting himself after only one or two laps. Later, when he was stronger, he began to run around the hospital grounds. His doctor gave him the helmet, a lightweight biking model, then, asking him to wear it when he ran—just in case.

He put it on his head now, waved at the night nurse, and headed for the door of the hospital. Outside, he stashed the plastic thing behind some hedges before running through the front gates and turning to the right—there were some nice hills around the zoo and he was looking forward to the exercise...

Chapter 1

Less than fifty miles south of the hospital, a battered old Chrysler delivery truck rumbled out of the driveway of Tijuana Hospital. In its bed was a load of highly radioactive Cobalt-60 bound for Mexico City and a waste disposal center.

It never made it that far.

The drivers made their way down a variety of busy and deserted roads before stopping at a gas station in Hidalgo Province, there, they met three men.

"*¿Lo tienes?* Do you have it?" the tallest of the men asked in crude Spanish delivered with an equally crude accent.

"*Si.*" The senior driver, a fifty-year-old with twelve children, stepped forward. "You have our money?"

"Of course." The man motioned and a second man handed him a sheaf of currency. "As agreed." He handed the money to the older driver who immediately began to count it. "You know what to tell the authorities?"

"Si," the older man nodded, dividing the bills into two piles and handing one to his assistant (also his senior son-in-law). "We fell asleep here and when we awoke…" He made a disappearing motion with his hands. "The truck was gone." He leaned forward, eyes fixed on the tall man. "I will get my truck back, right?"

"Your truck *and* cargo will be found by the authorities very soon." The man clapped the driver on the shoulder. "You have my word on that."

"Good." The driver nodded. "It would be difficult to make a living without the truck." He motioned his assistant toward the restaurant at the back of the gas station and turned to join him before stopping and turning back toward the tall man, "I hope I can be of use to you again sometime soon."

"I hope so too, my friend." The tall man smiled and motioned for one of his companions to climb into the truck. "I very much hope it works out that way."

Chapter 2

"How many miles this morning, Mr. Kelly?"

Each of the SEALs in Team Six had been given a cover name and background to use in their dealings with anyone outside their own chain of command. Randall 'Flame' McDonnell's was Brian W. Kelly, a swabbie who had fallen (or jumped—the Navy had never been sure) from the deck of the *Reagan* in 2011.

"I did about ten, Doc." Flame shrugged. "I'd have liked to do twenty or so but I had to get back here to see you." He looked at the medical officer. "I hope you have good news for me."

"The nurse tells me you aren't sleeping at all well." He shuffled some papers. "Nightmares, she says." He looked at Flame. "Is that true?"

Another shrug. "Sometimes."

"And your sense of taste? Is that still acting oddly?"

"I guess you could say that." Flame smiled ruefully. "I can't taste sweet stuff at all—ice cream, chocolate bars…" He shrugged. "They're no good at all." He grinned. "I'm kind of wondering what beer will taste like."

The doctor stood up and stood in front of his patient, carefully examining the now-healed scar on his head. "How about your head?" He gently traced the scar with a finger, noting the new hair growth around it. "Any pain? Do you see things out of the corner of your eye? Hear odd noises?"

Flame shook his head.

"You're sure? You've never heard someone or something that isn't there—or failed to hear someone who is?"

"Not that I'm aware of."

"I see…" The doctor nodded and returned to Flame's chart. "I think you're healthy enough to go on convalescent leave." He looked into Flame's eyes and smiled. "Get you away from that night nurse."

"I'd rather go back to my unit…"

"I can't do that—not yet, maybe not ever." The doctor shook his head. "You had a very serious head wound—your skull was broken and bits of bone penetrated your brain. It's a miracle that you can stand much less run--we have to be absolutely sure that you are completely healed before we can send you back to duty." The doctor made a final note. "Take your leave, visit your home, see your friends, then come back here in thirty days and we'll see what we see."

"Whatever you say, Doc." Flame stood.

"Orders will be at the nurse's station." The doctor stood and offered his hand. He was an old Navy hand and knew that Flame was more than he appeared—the flimsiness of his personnel file and the numerous scars on his body proved that. "Have a good rest and come back fit—I'll do everything for you that I can."

"Thanks, Doc." Flame shook his hand. "Can't come soon enough for me."

And then he was in the hall, wandering back to his room and thirty days leave that he had no idea what to do with.

***

On the other side of the border, the Mexican authorities announced that the truck holding the missing Cobalt-60 had been found and the four petty thieves who had stolen it arrested. All of the radioactive material was, they said, safe.

Of course, in Mexico, one can buy anything—even the assurances of the authorities…

Chapter 3

Flame, with nothing better to do, took the doctor's advice and went home—which, to him, meant the Naval Base at Dam Neck. He had hoped that the rest of the members of SEAL Team Six—or DEVGRU or whatever acronym they were using now—would be around, waiting on a new assignment.

None were, so Flame—using his Brian Kelly ID, checked into the BOQ and got to work.

He knew that the doctors didn't want to clear him for duty—that had been made perfectly clear to him in early in his stay at the Balboa Naval Hospital. The doctors had been terrified to allow him to run or work out with free weights—they were sure that he was too weak for such activity and would hurt himself further.

Flame had, of course, ignored them and started running in the hospital halls and doing pull-ups with the aid of his bed frame. The screeching nose of metal on wall bothered some of the other patients, several of whom were senior officers. When they complained, the doctors suddenly decided to allow Flame to run outside the building—safe in his little plastic helmet.

Home now (in SEAL terms) there was not a soul who could tell him what he could—and could not—do in his exercise routine. He used that to his advantage.

He started with easy runs—ten miles along the beach followed by an hour of weight training, lunch and then another ten miles up along the roads that surrounded the base. He did his best to work himself to the edge of exhaustion before hitting the sack.

It didn't work. He kept having the dreams. Always the same. Always inside that same Mexican shithouse and always ending up in front of the same damn door. The door into blackness.

The door of death.

He moved to thirty miles a day—fifteen in the morning and fifteen in the evening. He spent the remainder of his time utilizing the base's fully equipped weight room (doing so during off-hours, both to avoid having SEAL trainees asking questions, and to avoid going to sleep and suffering through the dream again).

It took time but eventually he regained most of the muscle mass he had lost while in the hospital and rounded into the kind of shape that many of the trainees would have traded everything they owned to match.

But he still wasn't sleeping.

He began to prowl the internet, looking through online stores to find things that interested him or might be cool to send to his buddies on the other side of the world. He purchased large quantities of various chocolate bars (which he could no longer enjoy) and sent them to the team who, he had learned, were somewhere in Afghanistan where such items were considered 'luxury goods' and hard to come by.

He found a place in Texas selling Dragon Skin armor and conductive cooling vests. He'd heard of such things—you wore them tight against your skin and they drew heat away from your body, slowing dehydration.

He knew the guys could use the gear. He also knew that the Navy wouldn't be buying anything like it for years. He ordered one for each of his buddies and included the man called Priest who, in his absence, had become part of the team.

He ordered a final set in his own size—although he had begun to doubt that he would ever use it. If he didn't kick the dreams he was sure he'd be kicked from the military—no matter what kind of shape he worked himself into.

By the beginning of his third week of leave he decided to try something different—he began to take time away from the sameness of beach runs and weight rooms. He made his way to Virginia Beach where he could prowl the sands and bars for willing little playmates for a night of rest and recreation in a rented room at the Sea Breeze Motel.

They were easy to come by—and always went away contented after a night of athletic sex.

Oddly, not one of them had red hair.

The change in routine helped a little—Flame still had the dream most nights but now it wasn't quite so intense. He still found himself in front of that door, but now he always knew it was a dream—one which he could escape by willing himself back to consciousness and away from whatever waited for him on the other side of that dark portal.

Chapter 4

Dana Morton was bored. This was her third night at the Calypso and her target had yet to show up.

My contacts must have been wrong, she told herself as she sipped a glass of ginger ale. *There are no SEALs here—just a bunch of wannabes and a lot of college kids who aren't old enough to know the difference!*

She been propositioned a couple of times—her youthful blonde looks practically guaranteed that would happen—but she'd fixed the offending males with her best withering glare and they'd melted back into the crowd, licking their wounds.

I can't stay here forever. She finished her drink and motioned for another one. *If he doesn't show up soon, I'll have to try a different...*

A tall, redheaded man wearing jeans and a t-shirt stepped into the bar.

That's him! Dana let her eyes roam over the six foot four mass of alpha male who strode into the room. *He looks healthy enough...* She fixed her gaze on his face and head, looking for... *There's the scar!* She bit her lower lip. *Not too bad—it'd be worse if he had more of a tan...*

She studied his gait. *No sign of a limp.* Her source had informed her that the target was running twenty to thirty miles a day and dead-lifting quite a lot of weight. *He certainly looks like he's ready to go.* She nodded to herself. *Yeah, I think he'll do.*

Dana dumped a bill on the table and stood, just as the redheaded man picked his target—a nineteen-year-old college girl in skin-tight short-shorts and halter top.

Yeah, she watched him say a few words to the girl who seemed a little weak in the knee as she stood and took his arm. *He'll do.*

Dana left the bar moments before Flame and the girl did.

***

Flame noticed the girl eyeing him as he walked into the Calypso. *Not bad looking,* he told himself as he gave her the once-over. *Real blonde—not a bleach job—good figure.* Her blue eyes swept over him—then pointedly turned away.

Flame was used to women checking him out. He was a good-looking man and knew that the ladies liked both his face and his muscular build.

This one was different. *She looks as if she's sizing up a prize bull.* Flame didn't like that look—and found another girl not far away—another blonde, much younger and much more skimpily dressed. By the time he reached his new target, the laser-eyed girl had disappeared from sight.

Flame and his new, curvy blonde conquest-to-be followed mere moments after.

Flame had the dream again that night—reacting violently enough that the girl fled the room before he was completely awake.

***

Another week passed. Labor Day was on the horizon and afterwards, most of the girls would disappear from the beach until next summer. Flame's leave was nearly over—and he knew that he would have to face a future that seemed to promise nothing but boredom.

They're never going to let me back in the Teams, he told himself. *I could lie about the dreams, lie about everything going on in my head—but if I did that I'd be putting my brothers in jeopardy.*

He knew he couldn't do that no matter what it cost him to avoid it.

I'll have to accept whatever the doctors say. He shook his head. *And that means I have no future in the Teams.*

He got his orders that day—orders to report to the Naval Hospital in San Diego for final evaluation.

Should I go? Maybe bring a lawyer and a doctor of my own?

He wished Manny was around—Manny would know what to do—but the big Jewish SEAL was in action with the rest of the team In fact, unknown to Flame, Manny was dead—killed by a Taliban bitch deep in the wilds of Afghanistan.

Flame tossed the orders on the bed and took a long walk. The base was active enough, with at least two bricks training and a new bunch of recruits working up alongside them.

Abruzzi! Flame thought. *Chief Abruzzi will know what to do.*

It didn't take long to find the old salt. He was hectoring a bunch of new recruits when Flame tracked him down on the beach. At the sight of the younger man's face, Abruzzi sent the newbies off on a five-mile run so he could give Flame his undivided attention.

The veteran SEAL deserved that much.

"So that's the story, Chief," Flame said as he looked the old man in the eyes a few minutes later. He had been careful not to tell the trainer anything classified—only filled him in the injury he'd suffered (without telling him where, when or how he got it) and his certainty that the Navy would decide to discharge him from the service.

"Is there any way I can beat this?"

"Damn, boy!" the old man looked into Flame's eyes. "I thought you were a SEAL." He spit into the sand and turned to walk away. "I thought you knew better than that."

Flame sat for a long moment—then nodded slowly. He did know better. SEALs did what they were told—even when they didn't like the orders. He watched the old salt trot up the beach, then turned and walked back toward his room.

A plan formed in his mind—a sure way to avoid the empty life that he knew was waiting for him.

Much later that night, Flame had the beach all to himself. He looked out to sea and saw his first target. It was a platform floating some fifty yards from the beach. Flame knew that it was held in place with chains and concrete anchors that had enough slack to let the thing rise and fall with the incoming tide. He'd swum to and from the thing for as long as he'd been a SEAL—after all, SEALs swam—and this platform was one of the places they learned how to swim properly.

He took a long moment to survey the scene. It was quiet and very peaceful. A sliver of moon lit the unmoving face of a very calm stretch of water. Flame remembered how it had looked when they'd dropped Bin Laden into the sea. It had been a rougher sea then—only to be expected since they were far out at sea—where this was just a protected bay.

I'm wasting time, Flame thought. *It's time to get to it.* He sat down on the sand and pulled off his trainers and sweats, neatly folding the pants and shirts before laying his shoes on top of them and pushing himself upright. *Time to go.* He walked toward the water, breathing deeply, filling his lungs with the air they would need for the first part of the swim. When he was sure he was fully oxygenated, he blew his lungs flat and slipped into the water, taking one last gulp of air just before his fingertips hit the water.

He grimaced a bit when as the liquid slid over him—it was colder than he'd expected this close to the end of summer—but then he felt a wry smile cross his lips. *What does it matter?*

Cold was good; it would give him focus.

He stretched and began the pull into the dark water ahead. He didn't look from side to side—SEALs never did—they trusted their brothers to keep up.

Twenty yards in and the muscles in his arms were starting to warm up with the exertion. He knew the platform was another twenty or thirty yards away—and he trusted himself to stay on line for the thing. Orienteering underwater is a bitch without any guidelines or lights but Flame had always had the knack. He had the direction firmly planted in his mind and he knew he wouldn't miss the platform—he had never missed in any of the training swims he had done over the years and he wasn't about to start now.

Sure enough, his fingers touched one of the chains holding the platform in place just about the time his brain said they should. He climbed up the chain and onto the platform, drawing in a deep breath and looking at the calm waters that surrounded him. To one side he could see the lights of Norfolk and, closer, Virginia Beach. He wondered if any of the pretty girls he had smiled at would remember him—and decided it didn't really matter.

I wasn't made for that, he told himself. *I was made to be a killer of men—a defender of my country.* He had spent years forging himself into the weapon that now stood on the platform—a weapon that his superiors had decided was no longer capable of accomplishing its missions.

There was nothing left for him to do.

He dove back into the water and began to swim—away from the beach.

Just over an hour later he stopped for a breath, treading water as he looked around. *I'm pretty far out.* He could barely make out the beach he had started from. *I wonder if I can make it to the other side.* He didn't think so—and he had no idea what he would do if he suddenly discovered he could.

He continued his swim, putting more space between him and the beach. It was almost out of sight now—a mere glimmer of sand in the dim moonlight.

I've almost got this done, Flame nodded to himself. *Just keep on going and sooner or later, I'll get too tired to continue and just quietly sink down into the sea...*

An altogether fitting end for a failed Navy SEAL.

"What the hell are you doing, buddy?"

The voice came from somewhere close. Flame stopped and treaded water as he searched for the source.

"Don't you know that SEALs always swim with a buddy?"

"Where are you?" Flame tried to pinpoint the voice. "I can't see you!"

"Doesn't matter, does it." The voice had a hint of humor. "Question is, why the hell are you just giving up?"

"I'm not giving up!"

"Don't give me that shit."

Flame heard the disapproval in the voice, and thought for a moment that he recognized it. *It sounds like Manny,* he thought. *But Manny's on the other side of the world!*

"Now get yourself turned around and head back to shore." There was that familiar hint of humor again. "SEALs—especially SEALs from Team Six, do not—I repeat—do not give up!"

He's right, Flame realized suddenly. *I shouldn't give up.* He still didn't know where the voice came from—but it really didn't matter. *I can't give up—it would dishonor the rest of the guys.* He shook his head. *What was I thinking?* He found the moon, used it to orient himself, then began the long pull back to the beach.

Abruzzi was waiting for him. The old chief didn't say a word, just handed Flame his clothes and turned away.

Chapter 5

Flame checked his reflection in the bathroom mirror. *Not too bad,* he thought. He'd had his hair cut before leaving Dam Neck, leaving it a little longer than regulation so it covered all but a tiny white 'V' of the scar tissue on his forehead—something that was hardly noticeable now that his tan had faded. He'd shaved very carefully and put on a brand new set of khakis—none of his older uniforms fit anymore. He carefully attached the bars, which identified him as a Warrant Officer W-2, and pinned the trident of the Teams on his breast.

Nothing else—SEALs did not wear brag rags.

Flame had been careful to choose a hotel situated close to the Pentagon so, when his watch showed that his appointment was only thirty minutes away, he used the time to walk to the designated entrance, taking a moment to look over the newly-dedicated Air Force memorial that stood nearby.

Nice enough, he thought as he looked over the soaring metallic sculpture. *If you like this kind of thing.* He turned his back on the statue and continued his walk to the Pentagon, effortlessly falling into a controlled pace that would get him to the proper door with plenty of time to spare.

A few minutes later—right on schedule—he was inside the heart of the US Military, being guided to the 'B' ring by a rather young lieutenant JG. "Did you know that you can get to any point in the Pentagon in seven minutes or less?"

"No, sir."

"It's a byproduct of the shape." The young officer motioned to the building around him. "There's a complicated formula that explains it all," he grinned. "But I don't really understand it."

"Yes, sir."

"The office you're looking for is right ahead." The lieutenant came to a halt and showed his pass to a Marine manning a security checkpoint. "Do you know who you're to see, Mr. Kelly?"

Flame was still using his cover name—and showed the visitor pass with that name to the Marine. "All I know is what's in my orders, sir."

"I see." They stepped through a metal detector and, when it didn't react, turned to the right. "Well," the lieutenant motioned to a door just ahead. "This is the office indicated on your papers." He stopped and smiled at Flame. "I hope they treat you well," he held out his hand. "I figure you probably deserve it."

"Thank you, sir." Flame shook the man's hand. "I'm not so sure of that—but it's nice of you to say."

"Smooth sailin', SEAL." The man stepped away, tossed a salute at Flame. "And keep your head down."

Flame returned the salute before turning to the office door. There was no metallic plaque alongside to indicate who resided here.

Doesn't really matter, Flame told himself. *I don't know anyone in the Pentagon anyway.*

He was wrong—as he discovered when he pushed the door open and entered a small, ten by ten foot room.

"Good morning, Flame." Lt. Commander Michael 'Bone' Ballard rose from the desk. He'd been a chopper jockey at Bagram during the Team's first deployment to Afghanistan and had flown Flame and his brothers out of a few hot spots. Bone was scarecrow thin—but that's not where his nickname came from. No indeed. Then Lieutenant Mike Ballard had received it when his crew chief—a rather well built blonde E-6—noticed how quickly parts of him came to attention when she walked by.

The fact that the same thing happened any time a pretty woman—or a not-so-pretty but well-endowed woman—appeared ensured that the name would stick.

And stick it did.

"Morning, sir." Flame stood loosely in the middle of the room. He could have come to a precise brace if he wanted to—but didn't really see the need. SEALs weren't much on ceremony—and the Bone knew that. "Nice of them to assign someone like you to take care of this."

"You know why you're here?"

"Orders are clear." Flame caught and held the other man's eyes. "They're putting me on the Beach although I don't really know why."

"There's no choice, son." Ballard touched the pile of papers on his desk. "The doctors say that the plate they put in your head could cause all kinds of problems. You already know about the problems with your taste buds—that's brain damage all by itself. Then there're the dreams which you admit you're having nearly every night." He shrugged. "That could mean you're susceptible to aural and visual hallucinations, which, all by themselves, would disqualify you from active duty."

"Is that what all those tests in San Diego showed?"

"They showed enough to convince the medics that you would put your team at risk if they allowed you back into the game." Ballard shrugged. "You wouldn't want that."

"No sir," Flame shook his head. "I guess I wouldn't."

"We can set you up with a job that you *could* handle—training new recruits or holding down a desk somewhere." Bone smiled. "Maybe a job as a cook on a warship?"

"I hated that movie, sir."

"The girl was awful easy on the eye, though." Ballard looked into Flame's eyes. "I know this is tough—it's why I'm here doing it instead of some enlisted flunky for whom it would be strictly routine."

"I appreciate that, sir."

"You'll get a medical discharge—with a full pension."

"Money isn't that important to me, sir."

"Yeah," Ballard grinned. "That's what the admiral said you would say."

"The admiral, sir?"

"You know who I mean." Ballard told him. "He asked me to give you the vinegar—and pass you along to the honey."

"I don't understand…"

"You will." Ballard pushed a sheaf of papers to Flame's side of the desk. "For now, though, I need you to sign a whole mess of papers—they're all marked as to where you have to sign them." He shrugged. "Mostly they say that you'll keep your mouth shut—not write a tell-all book, not do a movie deal," he grinned. "Like all those other guys."

"I'm not like them, sir."

"We didn't think you were." He handed Flame a pen. "But I've got to get you to sign them anyway—you understand."

"I do, sir." Flame looked at the topmost sheet—it was a recitation of the Military Secrets Act, which reminded him that he was still required to keep his big mouth shut about all the things he had learned while part of SEAL Team Six.

He signed without hesitation.

Ten minutes, and thirty or forty signatures later—Flame had lost count—Ballard handed him a sheaf of papers in a plastic sleeve. "Everything you'll need is in here—your DD 214 and all your retirement and medical information. Just put them somewhere safe."

"I have a safe deposit box…"

"Use it." The officer stood. "But before you do that, go to room 1B726," he pointed to his left. "It's right down the hall—you can't miss it."

"And what am I doing there?"

"Meeting what might be your future." Ballard stuck out his hand. "I hope you make the right choice."

"Thank you, sir." Flame turned toward the door.

"Remember—1B726."

"Yes, sir."

***

Dana Morton jerked to attention as the buzzer on her desk went off. *He's on his way,* she realized. Mike Ballard had been told to warn her when he finished with O'Donnell and apparently he had done just that.

She mentally went through the ex-SEALs record, ticking off his strengths and preparing to deal with his weaknesses. *I don't know if I can work with him,* she told herself. *But the admiral thinks he's the best man available—and I trust the admiral.* She allowed the ghost of a smile to touch her lips.*Besides, this 'Randy O'Donnell' is not a political animal—that in itself will be a relief!*

Dana had recently lost positions that meant something to her due to the acts of 'politicals' she had been forced to deal with. She had promised herself that she wouldn't make the same mistake with this new venture.

There was a knock on the door…

"Come in." Dana forced her face to go blank, ready to go to work.

Randall 'Flame' O'Donnell filled the doorway.

God, he's a big man! Dana had seen Flame before—journeying to Virginia Beach for some reconnaissance. He'd been a hair thinner then—a little out of shape, she supposed—and on the make. She'd done her best to avoid his eye—she didn't want to start what might be a long partnership by rejecting him—but he turned away from her and picked one of the college-age beach bunnies on their last week of summer vacation.

He'd been imposing then—now, with his six foot four frame covered in two hundred forty pounds of very well proportioned muscle, he was something else.

She stared into his face for a moment, held by his bright green eyes and flaming red hair. Her eyes moved to the scar she knew dominated the right side of his forehead. *It's not too noticeable now,* she told herself. In fact, the white 'V' on his forehead was only a ghost of its former self now that his tan was mostly gone. She wondered what it would look like if he got angry.

"Mr. O'Donnell." She rose and held out her hand. "I have a proposition for you."

***

Flame was surprised by the girl he found in this new office—which seemed identical to the one he had just left. *I know her,* he thought, looking over the trim form of the blonde who stood from the desk and held out her hand.

"Mr. O'Donnell," she said as she stepped forward. "I have a proposition for you."

"Virginia Beach," he said in response. "The Calypso." He pursed his lips as he remembered. "You were checking me out pretty good as I came in." He shook his head. "Gave me the creeps."

"I'm sorry about that, Mr. O'Donnell."

"You know who I am?"

"I know who you are and what you were." The blonde kept her hand out. "And I think I can offer you a job that will allow you to use your rather unusual set of qualifications."

He shook his head, ignoring her hand. "I'm not looking for a job." He held up the packet of paperwork. "I'm retired now. Disabled—medically discharged."

"Mr. O'Donnell..." Her bright blue eyes seemed surprised. "I don't think you understand..."

"Lady, I don't know what you're selling." Flame shook his head in negation. "But whatever it is, I ain't buying—and unless somebody's got a good reason to keep me here..."

He turned toward the door. "I'm gone."

He ignored the pleading in her brilliant blue eyes and stepped out into the corridor, anxious to put this place—and what had happened here—behind him.

Chapter 6

"He turned me down flat, sir." Dana lifted her glass and drained the remaining scotch. "Told me he wasn't selling…" She caught herself—decided she wouldn't have a third drink. "…Wasn't *buying* what I was selling."

"Did he look fit?"

"Fit?" Dana stared at the man across the table. "He looked as if he could take King Kong two out of three falls!"

"Good." Admiral Dorrance sipped his own drink. "I'm glad he's recovered."

"Medics say he has brain damage. That he sees things, hears things…"

"The medics don't know shit." The admiral banged his glass down on the table. "They don't know what makes a man a man—and they never will." He looked into Dana's eyes. "Flame is just what you need on this new venture."

"He said 'no!'"

"Try again." The admiral took a last sip of his drink. "And I know just how you can stack the deck in your favor…"

***

In Chihuahua, a brand new truck pulled away from Hospital Cima, a load of radioactive waste—Cobalt-60 pellets from the hospital's radiology section—locked inside. It roared down the main road onto the highway to Mexico City, but before it had travelled fifty miles, it was forced to stop by an apparent accident.

"Can I help?" The driver was a young man who was studying to become an emergency services technician—he drove for the hospital during the day and went to school at night. He'd learned enough to know that the man lying beside and partially under the car that was blocking the road might be seriously injured.

"I have a radio inside. Let me call the authorities and…"

He got no further. Another man—unseen by the trucker—came up behind him before he could reach the cab and slid a rather sharp knife under his belt and into his kidneys.

The driver was dead before he hit the ground.

Instantly, the 'injured' man came to his feet and joined his companion. Together, they pulled the body to the side of the road before climbing into the two vehicles and pulling away from the site of the non-accident.

Sometimes you can get what you want in Mexico without paying anyone a cent.

Chapter 7

In Northern Virginia, it only took Dana a few minutes to find Flame. The big man had left his hotel room just after dawn and was taking his morning run along the George Washington Memorial Parkway. He'd gone about seven miles when Dana caught up.

"Get in," she told him as she pulled off the road onto the grassy verge where she paced him.

"Why?" Flame didn't slow down. "You've got nothing new to say to me."

"You owe it to me to hear me out."

"I don't owe you a thing!"

"Do you remember Waylon Griggs?" Dana gasped as she saw the Fort Marcy overpass approaching. She rolled back onto the road, cutting off a big Cadillac Escalade whose driver slammed his hand down on the horn, then popped back onto the grass after passing the overpass.

Flame reached her a moment later, this time coming to a stop.

"Griggs was a good man—one of the best." He looked her over, a different sort of calculation in his eyes this time. "What do you have to do with him?"

"He trained me—I ran back office for him when he was on an op." She looked into Flame's eyes. "He was my friend."

The big man looked at her for a long moment, then: "Okay, I owe any friend of Waylon Griggs at least a few minutes of my time." He opened the door of her car. "Where shall we talk? If you want to go to a restaurant or something," he smiled and sniffed his armpits, "you're gonna have to let me get a shower first."

"We can do that later." She put the car into gear and merged—more carefully this time—into traffic. "There's something I think you ought to see while we're out here."

***

"Manny's dead?" They had been only a few minutes drive from the entrance to Arlington National Cemetery. Dana had taken them to the right area before leading Flame to the new gravesite. "Nobody told me!"

"The doctors didn't want to upset you." Dana put a careful hand on his shoulder. "But I thought you should know."

"Damn!" Flame stared at the simple stone marker. "He was such a good guy!" He looked at Dana. "What happened?" He thought for a moment, then added: "If you can tell me."

"He was on a mission out of Camp Iron Man in Afghanistan. The team was looking for a new jihadist leader that had sprung up in the northern part of the country. They found him—but while they were searching the cave he'd hidden his shit in, one of his wives shot Manny a couple of times."

"I sent him some special armor…"

"The postmortem said it was flail chest." Dana told him. "The hadji bitch fired two rounds that hit Manny's chest point-blank at an angle that snapped four of his ribs off at the sternum." She made a motion with her hands. "After that, each breath, each movement, brought the jagged edges of the breaks in contact with his lungs—and he had to move to get out of the cave he and the others were trapped in." She looked into Flame's eyes. "He bled into his lungs until he lost consciousness due to blood loss. Then his lungs simply filled with fluid and blood and he drowned while waiting for the CASevac chopper."

"That sucks."

"It does." She waited in silence while he made his peace with Manny.

"Let's have that talk now." Flame turned and headed for the car. "I really feel the need to kill some folks—and I would much prefer to make sure they're jihadist motherfuckers!"

***

Dana took Flame back to the hotel and waited in the lobby while he showered and changed. She had been surprised by the change in his manner when she mentioned Griggs.

The admiral was right. She had seen the respect in Flame's eyes as soon as she mentioned her friend's name. *The SEALs really liked and trusted Lon—and my relationship with him gives me a bit of residual respect.*

She hoped it would be enough to convince Flame to work with her.

I need him, she knew. *I need him and his experience to keep my clients alive—and us in business long enough to establish ourselves.* Only then, she knew, could they make a difference—and have the opportunity to, in Flame's words, 'Kill more of those jihadist motherfuckers!'

It wasn't long before the massive redhead stepped out of the elevator and spotted her in the lobby. She stood and led him out to her temporarily parked car.

"You hungry?" she asked as they left the parking lot.

"Depends." She saw him give a lopsided grin. "Some kinds of food taste…" He shrugged. "Kind of odd to me now."

"How about Tex-Mex?"

"I think I can manage that." The grin reappeared. "Not too many beans, though."

"I know a place…"

Twenty minutes later they were sitting at a table in El Garage, eating chips and sipping out of tall boys.

"You know," Flame told her, hefting the beer, "this is the only thing that still tastes exactly the same to me." He took a swig. "Crazy, right?"

"Just proves your brain still knows what's important." Dana took a sip of her own.

"Maybe so." His look changed, became far more serious. "Now tell me what job it is you want to offer me."

"Okay," Dana took another sip then looked her companion in the eye. "First you should know something about me. You're going to have to trust me and you should know that the reason I'm doing this is that I fucked up badly."

"How so?"

"I trusted the system." She bit her lower lip lightly in a nervous motion. "My daddy was in Vietnam." She glanced at Flame. "Seventy-Fifth Rangers."

"Good unit."

"He did two tours in country—on his way home from the second tour he got strip-searched at Sea-Tac and spat upon by a couple of protestors. That convinced him not to re-up." She looked at Flame. "When I told him I planned to go into the CIA he advised me not to do so. He said that politicians ran the show to keep themselves at the top of the pile, and that they didn't care a rat's ass—his words, not mine—what happened to the people they were supposed to be protecting."

Flame didn't move, just watched as she continued.

"When I started working with Griggs, I thought my dad was wrong." She looked up. "Griggs was a good man and he always thought about the people he was trying to protect."

"He *was* a good man." Flame interjected. "The team liked working with him."

"It got him killed." She shook her head. "The people who were supposed to be covering him on that El Young raid screwed up—they let the girl get away and even when they got eyes on, they didn't react quickly enough to stop her from setting off the car bomb that killed all of them—even Lon."

"Is that why you left CIA?"

"I was kicked out of CIA because I ignored the orders of an incompetent political appointee and a son-of-a-bitch from the State Department." She glared at Flame. "They 'promoted' me to NSA where I got screwed by a political manager because I wouldn't give him information he could use for his guy in the goddamn election!"

"Okay. You trusted the wrong people; that *was* a screw-up." He looked at her. "What makes the new job different?"

Dana nodded and took a swig of the beer. "I love this country—and I still want to help protect it." She looked at Flame. "I worry that assholes like the ones that screwed me and their boss are going to screw the pooch so bad that a lot of innocent folks will die." She hesitated for a second, then: "I want to start a private security firm, one that will specialize in protecting the right people—not the political bullshitters—when they have to go into a dangerous spot."

"And you want me to be the muscle?" Flame's tone was not encouraging.

"Look," Dana leaned forward. "I'm really good with intel and surveillance—but I can't do the kinds of things you and your buddies can. I need someone who can go out into the field with a client and make sure that he doesn't get kakked by the bad guys because he trusted the wrong people to watch his back."

"And who watches my back?"

"I do." Dana's voice was suddenly hard as iron. "Because you'll be my partner."

"Partner?"

"Co-owner of the firm I've started." She looked at him. "We'll make all the business decisions together—and we'll each run our own piece of the operations side." She raised an eyebrow. "That work for you?"

"Maybe." Flame took a swig of his own drink. "I assume you still have some contacts inside the intel community that you can turn to when you need them."

"One or two that I trust."

"Satellite and surveillance?"

"Again, one or two."

She saw him consider the possibilities and took the opportunity to finish her beer as a waitress showed a new party to the table just behind theirs. There was a young, rather frightened looking woman, three kids between two and seven years old and a large man who sported even more tattoos than Flame.

One of the kids—the seven year old—hesitated sliding down the seat of the booth they'd been shown to. The man growled a curse and backhanded the kid, the force of the blow knocking him against the wall.

Flame was on his feet before the kid started crying.

"What do *you* want," the tattooed man sneered at Flame. "You don't like the way I treat my kids?" He looked Flame up and down. "You a pig or something?" The man produced a butterfly knife, whipped it around his hand. "I don't like pigs."

Oh shit, Dana thought. *What is he going to do?* She looked around. *Do I need the cops? Should I call 911?*

"Don't hit the kid again." Flame kept his voice low enough that Dana could barely hear the words. "Don't hit any of the kids again."

"Get the hell out of here!" The big man held the knife at his side, blade toward Flame. "Who the hell do you think you are?!"

"I'm an angry man." Flame leaned forward. "Angry at the world." He shook his head. "Don't make me take it out on you." He raised an eyebrow. "You hearin' what I'm saying?"

The big man bristled—but made no overt move, just glared at Flame.

Who deliberately turned his back and took a step toward Dana.

As he did so, the tattooed man thrust hard with the butterfly knife, aiming it at Flame's kidney.

It never made contact. Flame had been expecting that kind of a move and, in a lightning-quick move, turned and grabbed the wrist of the man's knife hand. Dana could see the muscles on Flame's arm go rock hard as he closed his hand on that wrist, squeezing tighter —and tighter—and tighter.

The tattooed man's face changed. He tried to pry Flame's hand loose, tried to scratch at the bigger man's face.

All to no effect. Flame kept squeezing as the man struggled until, with a shockingly loud *crack*, something in the man's hand broke and the knife fell to the floor.

"Remember what I told you," Flame said, still gripping the man's twitching wrist. "Remember."

Then he released the man's hand and, without a look back, slid back into the seat across from Dana.

"I'm in on two conditions," he told her as he sat back down.

Dana let out a breath she hadn't realized she was holding. "What are they?"

"One: we concentrate on anti-terrorism and related security jobs—no hand-holding for mid-level politicos taking pleasure trips to 'inspect' hotspots."

"Precisely what I had in mind."

"Two," he looked her up and down. "How much money have you put into this?"

Dana was surprised. *Why does he need to know that?* She looked at him, read nothing in his face. *Is he trying to calculate a salary?* She doubted that. He really didn't seem to care about money. *Then why?*

Only one way to find out.

"I put in every cent I had saved and all the money I inherited from my dad." She looked into his eyes. "Just over a hundred thousand—enough to rent an office and pay for utilities for a few months."

"A hundred grand." Flame nodded. "Okay, you'll have my bank draft for the same amount by tomorrow afternoon."

"But…" Dana was confused. "I didn't ask…"

"Partners, you said." He signaled to the waiter for more drinks. "Equal partners." He smiled. "Gotta share the costs," he raised an inquiring eyebrow, "don't we?"

As they shook hands, the tattooed man limped past the table—carefully avoiding Flame's eyes as he left the restaurant.

Nobody paid him the slightest bit of attention—and nobody offered to help.

Chapter 8

As Flame and Dana started on their second round of drinks, two very different individuals sat down at a somewhat shabbier restaurant on the other side of the continent.

"*¿Tenemos suficiente?* Do we have enough?" Raphael Manuelo Mapache, with the blood of the Apache running through his veins, was ageless, his face carved and pitted by years in the sun. His companion, Matias Blanco was, by comparison, pale and smooth-skinned with soft flesh that showed every one of his fifty-five years.

"One more shipment," Blanco sighed. "We need at least one more shipment to get the desired result."

"That will be difficult," Mapache settled back into his seat and motioned for service. "There are no more shipments scheduled." He shrugged. "This is not a rich country—the radiation treatment is not a common one."

"What about the other side of the border?" Blanco paused as the waiter arrived and put two glasses down on the table. "You know I cannot drink this," he told his companion as the waiter walked away. "Why did you order it?"

"Do not worry," the leather-skinned Mapache told him as he drained the first glass. "It will not go to waste."

"I see…" Blanco, a convert to the religion of peace, often wondered why Allah did not strike down men like this Mexican who sneered at his laws. *But if he did*, the Argentinian told himself. *Who would we use to do the work that needs doing?*

He allowed himself a small smile, then said: "You have not answered me—is there a supply of the material on the other side of the border?"

"It would not work." Mapache made a negating gesture. "We can pay off the *federales*—they expect as much—but if we raided a hospital in the United States," he shrugged, "there would by many questions asked." He leaned toward the smaller man. "Questions that might reveal things about the other missing shipments…"

"We *must* get the needed material!"

"There may be a way." Mapache picked up the second drink. "It could be expensive."

Blanco smiled. *It is always money with men like these— as if it will save them from the anger of God!*

Aloud, he simply said: "Money is not a problem."

Chapter 9

Flame was shocked at how much the world had changed for him when he followed Dana out of the commercial flight that had taken the two of them to Baghdad International. *It's like I've been wearing sunglasses and just took them off!* The past few weeks setting up the new security firm had been busy ones for Flame. *I needed the work.* He hadn't had a dream in all that time and now, as he scanned the battered arrivals building and the checkpoints that were set up at every access point, he felt his old self. *Everything is so clear—so sharp.*

His mind reeled with memories of this place. *It even smells familiar;* he followed Dana into the customs office. *Garlic and cinnamon and sweat.* He smiled. *Never changes.*

The customs inspector passed them without any problems—ignoring the sidearm that was part of Flame's checked luggage. *Everyone here goes armed,* Flame remembered. *Mostly with rifles that they fire into the air for no good reason at all.*

The first thing on Flame's list was to get a decent rifle— and enough ammo for the task he and Dana had undertaken.

"I'll go see one of my old buddies," he told her. "Get the stuff we're gonna need."

"Good," she said as the cab they had hired dropped them in front of the hotel. "I'll set up the commo rig while you're gone." She glanced at her watch. "Don't take too long—the rendezvous is only about half a day away."

"No sweat." He gave her his luggage—sans the sidearm, which he took out and slid into his belt. "I shouldn't be more than a few hours."

"See you later, then."

As Flame hailed a ride, the muezzin sang out the first call to prayer. *Yep*, Flame thought. *I'm back in hadji country.*

***

"I'll be happy to set you up, Flame—what do you need?"

Jason 'Scud' Johnson had been Marine Recon during the occupation. When American forces pulled out, he'd stayed on and found work as a private contractor, first with Blackwater and later, with MVM, Inc. They needed someone like him to be head honcho for the Latin American mercenaries they preferred to use as cannon fodder.

Flame had met him back in the day and knew he'd have what was needed for his trip outside the Green Zone.

"Just the usual, Scud." Flame shrugged and looked around. "I was able to bring my sidearm through security—but I need a long arm and some ammo."

"American rifle?"

"Maybe." If all went the way Dana had laid it out, Flame wouldn't have to fire a shot—but it never hurt to be prepared. "What do you have?"

"Got a couple of M4's." Johnson was a small man—just over the Marine height minimums. "But they're pretty burned out—barrels need replacing."

"No." Flame shook his head. "If I've got to shoot, I'd like to hit what I aim at."

"I read you." Johnson turned away for a moment, rummaged around in a cabinet set low to the floor. "How about this?" He turned with a spotless AK-47 in his hand.

"Let's see." Flame took the weapon (which did not have a magazine inserted), checked the chamber to make sure there was no round in it, then broke it down for a quick look.

"Russian made, I see." The weapon had a thick-milled receiver end, far superior to the stamped pot metal the Chinese made. The barrel was chromed inside and the stock was Rynex rather than wood.

Flame checked the action—it was smooth—glass on glass.

"Not bad." He put the rifle down on the table. "What do you want for it?"

"Five thousand."

"I only want to rent it," Flame shook his head. "Not have it plated in gold!"

"Okay, okay," Johnson waved a hand. "As you're an old friend…" He grinned. "And as you give me your word I'll get the piece back…" He held out a hand. "Two thousand, five hundred."

"Throw in a couple of hundred rounds of ammo and a few clips and you have a deal."

"Done!" Johnson's smile widened. "And just because this has been so pleasant, I'll even throw in a couple of grenades!"

"Fragmentation?"

"What other kind is there?"

The two men laughed, then: "Okay, Scud—now that we've settled that—what kind of four-wheel drive vehicles do you have that I can rent for a day or two?"

Chapter 10

Dana had been surprised at how cold it was in Baghdad. *I always thought of this place as a desert,* she thought. *But they do get a little bit of winter, which is why the temperature is less than fifty degrees.* She smiled. *Still better than D.C. It's snowing there…*

Flame had warned her to bring warm clothes and he was, after all, the expert. He was out hitting up some of his old buddies for the gear they would need to finish the operation. Her job was to set up a base and work out a communications set-up that would allow them to stay in contact without interfering with or being overheard by any of the local operators.

Both would be important if they wanted to work here again in future.

She had acquired a complete AN/PRC-152 handheld radio set-up—including a base transmitter/receiver and Sierra programmable encryption—before leaving the states. If it worked as advertised, it would have enough range to keep her in contact with Flame throughout the mission. If it didn't…

He returned to the suite they had rented in the Palestine Hotel just after the first call to prayer. He had a large metallic case slung over his shoulder, which told her that he'd been successful.

"No problem getting what we needed." He shut the door behind him, glancing over his shoulder to make sure no one was watching. "How's the comm coming?"

Flame had argued against using any of the hotels in the Green Zone because he knew all were full of reporters and film crews. She argued that its location alongside the Tigris would give them a good line of sight for communications—and that was more important than avoiding the leeches that fed the never-ending thirst for twenty-four hour news.

She had the stronger argument—which is why they were in the Palestine.

"Here." She handed him an earpiece. "It's the same kind you've been using in the Teams—just touch to activate."

He inserted the plastic device, tapped it once. "Like that?"

In answer, she picked up the headset and mike from the table and tapped it twice.

She smiled when he winced.

"What do you think?" she asked, and handed him the transceiver that fed the earpiece. "Keep that within about twenty feet and it'll work just fine."

"Encryption?"

"Cyclical." She patted the unit. "The NSA might decode it—but we don't care about them."

"Sounds good." He turned to the big case that he'd dumped on one of the beds. "I'll head out just before sunset so I can clear the checkpoints—that's assuming the pick-up is still on for tonight?"

"No changes."

"Good." He pulled out five magazines for the AK-47 and several boxes of Russian-made bullets. "Then I guess it's time for me to start earning my money." He started loading rounds into the mags, making sure each seated properly. "I am earning money, am I not?"

"I guess." Dana shrugged and continued fiddling with the radio system. "We'll have to get the bosses to work out the pay scale." She smiled. "Maybe back in that El Garage place." Her grin widened. "I kind of liked their burritos."

"Me too. Their beer wasn't bad either." Flame finished with one magazine, started on a second.

"What did the burrito taste like to you?" Dana usually avoided personal questions with Flame—but he seemed to be in a good mood.

"Peanut butter and jelly." he shook his head. "And you don't want to know what the beans tasted like!"

Flame figured to head out just before the next call to prayer. He put the rifle back in its case and added the loaded magazines, grenades and radio gear. Clicking the case locked, he stripped off his shirt and donned his body armor. A lightweight jacket (from the Big and Tall shop in Georgetown) went over the armor, disguising it to some extent. His Sig Sauer P226 went into a cross-drawer holster on his belt and a ka-bar combat knife slid into a sheath that was an integral part of the armor's spine.

When he was done he was running light—less than thirty pounds of gear. He shook things down, took a moment to see that everything was in place, then shouldered the rifle case and headed for the door.

"I'll check in when I clear the final checkpoint," he told Dana as he headed out.

"Right—and again when you reach the rendezvous point." She smiled at him. "Don't start a war—please?"

"I'll do my best." He gave her his best wicked grin. "But I can't make any promises."

And then the door was closed and he was gone.

The elderly Land Rover he'd gotten from Scud was the perfect car for the mission—assuming that it ran as advertised. The engine sounded healthy enough and the ride back to the hotel proved it to solid enough that Flame had hopes. Besides, it was battered enough to fit in with all the other cars on the road in Baghdad—with luck no one would expect a foreigner to be driving such an ugly car.

Twenty minutes later, he activated his radio and reported himself clear of the city. The guards at the checkpoint really didn't give a shit about anyone leaving the Green Zone—their concerns centered on those entering—and what they might be carrying.

Flame would deal with that aspect of the mission later. For now he speeded to the northwest. He had about a hundred and fifty klicks to cover before daybreak.

He found himself enjoying the experience.

I can't believe I'm back in the sandbox, he thought as he sped down one of the recently repaired highways that carried most of the city's northbound traffic. *It's too bad Sergeant Neff and his unit are gone—I could have gotten some top-rate gear from them, although this...* He patted the case beside him. *Ought to do just fine.*

The return to Iraq had affected him strangely. He'd thought himself fully recovered from the aftereffects of his head wound right up until he deplaned at Baghdad International. As soon as he stepped into the open air everything became clearer—more precise. It was as if his senses had been boosted somehow.

It's because I'm back on duty—sort of, at least, he told himself. *My old habits of observation just snapped back into place.* It was a good thing—a thing that might keep him alive if this mission went to shit.

Flame crossed the Tigris on a rickety concrete and wood bridge and turned more westerly. He wanted to be at the rendezvous location with time to spare. It never hurt to have a good hide to check things out—and he planned to be ready and under cover in plenty of time to do just that.

***

Dana watched her partner's progress on the GPS system that was part of the comm unit. Satellite coverage over the sand box was quite efficient and she was able to watch him move swiftly along the paved road that paralleled the river.

It'll get rougher when he goes off the road, she knew. *I'll probably lose the GPS then.* She bit her lip. *Wish I had a drone at my disposal—or a satellite overview.*

She knew that wasn't going to happen. *I'm independent, now.* She enlarged the image on her laptop. *For better or for worse...*

A glance at the TV—which she had left on with the sound turned down—showed her that things were heating up in Fallujah and Tikrit. *I hope our clients got out okay.* She and Flame had contracted to secure and escort a TV documentary crew that had been shooting footage in the Sunni-dominated regions of Iraq when things started going south.

Their own security guards—hired by the network they worked for—had fled when gunmen attacked a satellite station the news crew was using to uplink their material. The network, based in Germany, had asked the US for help—which had been denied due to the current American policy of 'no boots on the ground.'

The request had, however, been heard by other departments and offices—one of which seized the opportunity to suggest Dana's newly formed agency might be able to help.

Dana and Flame had been on a plane sixteen hours later.

Idiots should have left as soon as Al-Qaida militants began to appear in the streets. Dana knew. *Now they've lost their guards and their ability to contact their home base.* She glanced at the TV. *And soon they're going to have to duck both the militants and the Iraqi army! There are crazies on both sides who are going to shoot anything that moves.* She shook her head. *Including a harmless press contingent.*

The whole place is going to go south just like Syria did. Dana turned back to the computer and the swift-moving dot that was Flame. *I hope he finds those people and gets them out of there before that begins to happen!*

Chapter 11

It was full dark when Flame parked the Land Rover in a wadi on the east side of the Euphrates River. The trip had taken a bit longer than expected because the main highway had been crowded with Iraqi military vehicles moving toward Fallujah. Flame had been forced to use an alternate route, bypassing the city and ending up off-road about two klicks from his destination—a pumping station on the southeastern outskirts of Tikrit.

It was clear that the city was in turmoil—Flame could see tracer rounds cutting long arcs through the sky over the city. *Somebody is burning a lot of ammo in there,* he told himself. *Just like the old days.*

The meet was scheduled for sunrise and Flame's plan was to get there very early and find a spot where he could oversee as much of the area as possible without being seen.

He had long since lost commo with Dana—too much interference from the Iraqi military, which had some problems with communications discipline.

He knew that he'd have to make all the decisions.

His first was to park here. He knew that the Land Rover could get much closer to the rendezvous point—it handled well off-road—but it was noisy and noise carried amazingly well in the desert at night. Flame didn't have many advantages here—and he wouldn't throw one away just for the comfort of his clients. The TV crew could walk from the pick-up point to the car. The exercise, he was sure, wouldn't kill them.

Dana picked a good night for this, Flame told himself as he moved across the sand, barely glancing at his compass. *Moon's nearly full.* The ex-SEAL hadn't realized how much he'd come to depend upon the night vision gear that had become so much a part of the unit's tactical load-out. *SEALs own the night!* He remembered that oft-repeated phrase with a laugh as he looked around the brightly-moonlit landscape. *Just not a night like this!*

It was just as well. He made a mental note to acquire some night vision gear for future jobs and jogged toward the tracer-ceilinged city.

It took less than an hour to find the pumping station. Flame crept around the building making sure there were no guards, then, circling away from the structure, found a spot with enough elevation to give him a good look at the crew's back trail.

He scooped a shallow trench out of the sand, lay down inside, and pulled a desert-cammo ghillie cover over him.

Binoculars out, Kalashnikov ready, he settled in to wait.

***

The sun was just lightening the eastern sky when Flame saw movement to his front. *Could be them,* he thought, moving the binoculars to bear on the still-distant figures.

There were three people—two men and a woman—all loaded down with backpacks and carrying cases that, he was sure, were loaded with camera equipment and other gear.

Flame resisted the urge to shake his head. *The extra weight is tiring them—slowing them down.* He saw the fatigue as they moved toward him. *It would have been smarter to dump it all and just carry whatever they really needed.* Again he carefully did not shake his head. *Civilians never understand that—somewhere deep down they think every bit of the crap they carry is vitally important.* He watched them struggle along. *Nearly as important as their lives.*

Another movement drew his attention. It came from behind the trio of civilians. *Looks like they've got company.* He slid his binoculars to the new target. *Three men moving fast.* He studied the newcomers, noted the typical Iraqi clothing—and the even more typical armament. *They've got AKs and an RPG launcher.* He smiled. *I've seen that combination before!*

For the first time he wished he'd brought a scope-mounted weapon—but he knew such a rifle would have been a mistake. *I can't just shoot them on sight.* Dana had warned him to avoid that sort of thing. *Not until I can tell whether they're good guys or bad guys.* He clicked the safety of the AK-47 off. *I'll just have to wait and see...*

He knew that he wouldn't have to wait too long. The heavily loaded trio was almost to the pumping station now. The man in the lead looking for some sign of the help he'd been notified was coming.

I'm here, Flame thought. *Just get to cover and wait...*

He put the binoculars to one side and slid the Kalashnikov to his shoulder, clicking the selector switch to 'single shot.'

The metallic click echoed over the desert—but nobody heard it because it was drowned out by the sound of two AK-47s opening fire on full automatic.

Militants, all right. Flame nodded to himself as he watched the men chasing the trio open fire—in full 'spray and pray' form. *No fire discipline at all.* He rested the iron sights of his own AK on the leftmost figure, adjusted the aim slightly for distance and stroked the trigger.

***

Karin Hachtel was certain she was about to die. She screamed in fear as the men behind her began shooting and scrambled to follow her cameraman, Eric, as he ducked behind the cinder block wall of the pumping building.

"Stay here," he pushed her up against the building. "I'll get Dieter."

Karin huddled against the bricks, wondering how this had happened. *We're not supposed to get shot at!* She sucked in a long breath. *We're just reporting on the way Sunnis are treated now that the Shias are running the country.* She shivered as bullets hit the sand a few meters from the shelter of the building. *We're on their side!*

She saw a flash from a rise almost across from her. *That's odd.* She leaned forward, trying to see more clearly. *I wonder…*

There was another flash.

"There's someone over there!" She grabbed Eric by the arm. "I think he's shooting toward us!"

"I hope to God it's our new security team," the tall and slender Eric said, as he scrabbled for his camera. "Because if it's not, we are all going to die here."

"Look!" The third member of their team, Dieter, had pulled himself to the corner of the wall and was peering around it. "One of the men chasing us has fallen. The others..." He turned back to his two companions. "The others seem confused."

"I hope they stay confused." Eric began assembling his camera, then thought better of it. "Hey—while we have time..." He nodded at the river a few yards in front of them. "Perhaps we should cross?"

"Our contact said to wait here." Karin nodded toward the building. "By the pumping station."

"They didn't know someone was going to be shooting at us!" Eric zipped up his case. "Come on—we can't stay here!"

Karin shook her head—but crouched, ready to follow the tall man.

***

What are those idiots doing? Flame had taken down one of the men chasing the TV crew and, as he'd expected, the other two had frozen in place for a long second before dropping to the ground as they frantically searched for the location of this new player.

All they have to do is sit where they are, Flame had picked out his second target and had the sights set on the lump that he knew to be the other rifleman—when that worthy looked up, he would get a real eyeful...

But before that happened, the trio, who had been huddled in perfect safety against the pump house wall, began to move, heading toward the river at an angle that would—they hoped—keep the building between them and their pursuers.

Flame shook his head. *Idiots! As soon as they hit the water they're going to be visible—sitting ducks for those two hadjis.* He knew he should use them as bait—wait for his two targets to move to shoot the easy targets in the river—but he couldn't take the chance that his clients would get hit before he took down the shooters. *I'll have to act now.* He concentrated on the tiny target he had carefully centered in his sights. Flame stroked the trigger again.

The round hit the second rifleman on the highest point of his ass, sinking deep into the soft flesh and rewarding Flame with a scream of anguish—and a better target.

A third stroke left just the holder of the RPG.

Give up, asshole. The TV crew was halfway across the river now. *You can't win.* Flame kept his rifle zeroed in on the area he knew the third man was hiding in. *All you have to do is run away,* he smiled. *I won't shoot you.* The smile widened—hardened. *Really I won't...*

On cue, the man struggled to his knees, turned the rocket launcher toward Flame's position...

The SEAL was ready. His first shot took the man in the center of his chest. The second hit just under his right eye, drove into the brain, and exploded—accompanied by a stream of blood and grey matter—out the back of his head. The corpse stood erect for a long second...

Then tumbled backwards, the grenade firing straight up as a dead hand tightened on the trigger.

Flame watched the rocket motor fire as the round cleared the launcher. It went nearly a thousand feet straight up—then fell to a point only a few inches from its firing point—right into the stomach of the RPG operator. The resultant explosion, Flame thought, insured that if the bastard did indeed get to paradise, he probably wouldn't enjoy the virgins all that much.

***

Karin was almost out of the river when the explosion rocked the area around her. She looked back just in time to see the area beyond the pump station erupt in red-tinted sand.

"Our friend up there got all three of the men chasing us," Dieter shouted from behind her. "I told you we should have waited!"

"It's too late to worry about that now." Eric clambered up the bank and reached back to help Karin. "Where is our benefactor?"

"Over there." Karin saw a movement to their left and up the hill.

All three turned in time to see Flame rise from the ground like some warrior god of old.

Chapter 12

"This way!" Flame motioned for the three Germans to come up the hill toward him. "Hurry!" He kept his own eyes downrange—scanning the area for any movement.

"Come help us with the equipment!" That from the blond cameraman. "It's heavy!"

"Carry it or leave it!" Flame ignored the man and kept his attention on the landscape in front of him. "There might be others after you!"

"Pick it up, Eric." The woman had already hefted her own bag and case. "He's right!"

Flame heard the cameraman mutter something that was probably a curse before all three of the Germans managed to get grips on all of their their equipment and start climbing toward him.

"Land Rover is back there," he told the girl when she reached his position. "About two klicks that way." He jerked his head toward the wadi that hid the vehicle. "Go—I'll make sure we're clear and catch up with you before you get there."

"That way," the girl nodded. "Two klicks." She motioned for the others to follow. "Right."

Flame watched the three as they crested the hill and hurried down the back side to make sure they were on the right track.

They were.

His attention returned to the area before him. He could hear the sounds of gunfire in the city. *Small arms,* he noted. *Nothing heavy.*

That meant the militants didn't have any artillery in this area.

The Iraqi Army can stop this—crush them before they gain power. A wry smile crossed Flame's lips. *If they want to take the trouble to do so.* He remembered his own time in Fallujah and how difficult it had been to get any Iraqi—Sunni or Shiite—to do anything at all.

They'll let it fester. He knew that the black flag of Al-Qaida had already gone up over Fallujah. *Until they can't clean it out on their own.* He scanned the area around the pump house one more time. *Then they'll cry for us to help them.* He rolled up his ghillie cloak, put it into his pack and headed down his back trail, following the clear trail left by the film crew. *I wonder if we will?*

He broke into a lope, anxious to catch up before his wards did something stupid.

***

Karin kept Eric and Dieter moving in the direction the big American had indicated. She had been surprised to see just how big he was. *The man is a giant!* She shook her head. *Two meters tall at least! And those shoulders...*

She wondered what Eric was thinking. He'd been ready to challenge the man over his refusal to help carry the gear. *I'll bet he won't do that now that he's seen him up close!*

They'd been walking for nearly an hour now and Karin was surprised that the big American hadn't caught up. *I didn't hear any more shots—what could be delaying him?*

She started to turn around—and found the big man just a few feet behind her.

"You're still about a klick out." He shook his head. "You've got to speed it up."

"Help us with the equipment." Eric had jumped when the man had first spoken but now had himself under control. "It's too much for us to carry."

The big man ignored him. "I'm going on ahead to make sure the Land Rover is safe." He pointed slightly to his left. "Follow my tracks—I'll meet you before you get there."

Then he was gone—trotting across the loose sand away from them as silently as he had come up from behind.

Karin watched for a second, then lifted her box of equipment and followed along—faster now—she suddenly realized that she never wanted to disappoint this man again.

***

Flame didn't have to check his GPS to find the Land Rover—he knew where it was. He trotted at a comfortable pace after leaving the three Germans, not slowing until he was less than a thousand yards from the car. From there he moved quietly forward until he came to a slight rise in the Earth that gave him some cover. Once there he took out his binoculars and had a long look.

Nobody in sight, he thought as he scanned the area—and saw the scuffs in the sand he had cleared when he left the vehicle. *But someone has definitely been here.* He settled in and began to carefully search the area. *Now where are they...?*

One over there, he could just see the barrel of an AK peering out from a high point about fifty yards back on the other side of the wadi. *Tracks indicate there're at least two of you— where's your friend...* He smiled when he saw the edge of a scarf just visible behind the car. *Bingo!* Flame pushed himself back from the edge of the rise and began to move back the way he had come. *If I can just get the Germans to stay put long enough to allow me to handle this...*

The film crew, he soon discovered, hadn't gotten very far after he left them. He found them sitting in a circle 'resting' not two hundred meters from where he'd seen them last.

"I am sorry..." The dark-haired reporter hesitated, eyes on Flame. "What do we call you?"

"Call me Flame." He smiled, pulled off the cap he'd been wearing. "Everybody does."

"Good!" She smiled. "Then, Flame, I am sorry we have not yet reached the Land Rover. Eric," she nodded at the cameraman, "insisted we rest before moving any further."

"It's good you did." Flame squatted in front of them. "Two ragheads found the car and are waiting to ambush the driver when he gets back."

"What did you say?" Eric leaned forward, his eyes hot.

"I said there are two ragheads waiting to ambush us at the car."

"It is no wonder the Arab world dislikes you Americans so much." Eric sniffed. "Calling them names, assuming the worst of them!" He glared at Flame. "The men are Sunni tribesman—good people! I am sure they are merely waiting to see if the owner of the car needs any assistance."

"With their AK-47s ready to help him right out of this world." Flame shook his head. "Are you really that stupid?"

"I am not stupid—and you are wrong about these people!" Eric began to get to his feet. "I will prove it!"

"How do you plan to do that?" Flame figured he knew what the idiot had in mind but he was perfectly prepared to let him say it out loud.

"I will walk to the car and talk to these men." He stood up straight. "I will show you that they mean us no harm."

"Are you going to put the girl in jeopardy too?"

"Fraulein Hachtel believes as I do—don't you Karin?"

The reporter looked from the massive form of flame to the lanky Eric. "I am not so sure ..."

"Don't tell me you are beginning to believe all the propaganda!"

"Eric, they tried to kill us."

"Merely a misunderstanding of some kind." He shook his head. "I'm sure we could have worked it out."

"Sure," Flame interjected. "Right after they shot you full of holes."

"Those were foreign fighters—outsiders—the Sunni are good people." He turned in the direction of the car. "And I will prove it to all of you." He took a long stride forward, glanced behind him to see if the others were following, then, when he saw they weren't, shook his head and started walking in earnest. *He would show this arrogant American the error of his thoughts!*

Shit! Flame thought as the cameraman strode away. *I can't just let him get killed...* He looked at the two remaining Germans: "Stay here—both of you." He turned away. "Don't move!"

He wasn't sure they would do as he said—but he couldn't worry about that right now. Right now he had to get back to the wadi before that idiotic cameraman did.

He broke into a run.

Chapter 13

Dana stared at her laptop, willing it to show her Flame's signal. She'd lost contact with her partner soon after he crossed the Tigris River—there was too much interference caused by the government forces moving in the same area.

She had managed to track him for some time through the GPS transceiver on his Land Rover—but it hadn't moved in hours.

You're running out of time, Flame! She tried to will that thought to him. *Fallujah's going to hell and you might not be able to get back here if you don't start soon.*

She stared at the dot that marked his position. *MOVE DAMN YOU!*

***

Flame was running all out down a long winding pathway that had once been a tributary of the Euphrates. The entire area that had been chosen for the rendezvous and pick-up was full of wadis like this one—dried up streams and river outcroppings. Flame had parked the Land Rover in one such wadi—albeit one with a flattened, sloping side. He had chosen it to hide the vehicle from casual observation but kept it close enough to be useful.

It was just bad luck that the hadjis had stumbled across it.

Next turn I think, Flame was moving as quickly as was safe. He had scouted the area and knew that the long, winding track he was in rolled around behind and parallel to the one in which he'd parked the Land Rover. He had to reach that point before the German cameraman showed himself to the men watching the vehicle.

He didn't have much time.

He speeded up a little, willing to make a little noise if it got him into position on time. He turned a corner and put on the brakes—eyes wide. *Shit!*

Manny stood in front of him, an easy smile on his face. As Flame stared at him, his friend tapped his nose twice.

Flame suddenly smelled something.

Tobacco! Flame stopped and dropped into a crouch. *Somebody's smoking...* He searched for the source, forgetting about the impossible vision of Manny. *There!* He slowly moved to his right and slithered up the side of the wadi...

There was a man less than five feet in front of him, leaning against a rock and watching Flame's Land Rover from its cover.

There're three of them! Flame realized. *I would have run right past him if it hadn't been for...* He pushed that memory aside and took a long look around the little wadi. The other two Iraqis were right where he'd left them. *At least Eric the loudmouth hasn't gotten here yet.* He took a long look in the direction he'd left the German crew. *Any time, though.*

It was time to go to work. Flame drew the fighting knife from its scabbard on his back…

He studied the man in front of him. Smoking was frowned upon by most Muslims—but this man was old enough to have taken up the habit before its health risks were known. *Okay with me,* Flame thought. *Easier to find someone advertising their position.* He crawled up the back slope until he was only a couple of feet behind the man then, quickly and silently, he slipped his arm around the man's throat and drove the knife up and under his rib cage, the blade slamming into the Arab's heart and killing him in an instant.

Flame twisted once to make sure that there were no mistakes, then eased the unmoving body to the ground, wiping the blood from his knife as he did so. *That's one,* he told himself.

The second hadji was about thirty meters away, hiding behind another rock just to the east of the Land Rover. Flame returned to the wadi and made his way down the twisting channel until he estimated he was just beneath his second target. A quick peek over the ridge told him he was in the right position. *Don't let him get a shot off,* Flame told himself. That would complicate things.

He dropped his pack and wriggled up the slope, knife ready.

***

Eric Piper was panting as he approached the Land Rover. He'd gotten lost soon after he lost sight of the others, forcing him to circle a bit until he caught sight of the roof of the car just peeking over the edge of one of the countless wadis that wove in and out of this part of the desert.

Now to show that warmongering jackass that he's wrong! Eric had spent the last few months shooting footage of the Sunnis and while they hadn't exactly welcomed him and his crew with open arms, they hadn't fired at them either.

Until this morning. He remembered the men who had chased them out of Tikrit. *But they weren't really Sunnis,* he reassured himself. *They were foreigners—outsiders just interested in causing trouble.*

Like the big American...

Eric stood up straight and tall as he headed straight at the Land Rover. He'd show that redheaded bastard that violence wasn't the only way.

***

Flame watched as Eric strolled down the gentle slope toward the car. So did the hadji who had been hiding behind the vehicle. As Flame watched, the Iraqi clicked the safety off his AK and slowly stood up, glancing over his shoulder to the point where he knew his backup lay in wait—ready to help him shoot an unarmed man.

***

Eric saw the young man stand up from a place of concealment behind the car. *Natural enough,* he thought. *He was probably just sitting there, taking some sun.* Eric smiled at the thought. *I wouldn't mind having a day to sit around and relax.* He looked around. *Although I'd prefer it to be a bit warmer...*

The young man lifted an AK-47 and pointed it at Eric.

"No need for that." Eric lifted his hands to show that he had no weapons of his own. "I'm not going to hurt you." He smiled. "I'm your friend."

He saw the young man's hand tighten on the weapon's grip, saw his finger begin to squeeze the trigger.

Eric closed his eyes as a gunshot ripped through the little wadi, something hit his chest—and he fell to the ground, unconscious.

***

"Are you sure he will be all right?" Karin frowned in concern as Flame lifted the still form of Eric from the ground and pushed it into the back seat of the Land Rover.

The vehicle had suddenly appeared as she and Dieter waited alongside the equipment. She'd been afraid that it was the militants following them from the city but had soon realized it was Flame driving the thing.

With his help they'd quickly loaded the camera equipment into the vehicle's large boot, then jounced back over rough country until they rolled down a gentle slope into a fairly deep wadi. Eric was there, flat on the ground, out cold.

Less than ten feet away a young Sunni lay flat on his face, the back of his head a gaping, bloody hole.

"He discovered that he was wrong about the peaceful Sunni tribesman." Flame shook his head. "Fortunately, I was in a position to cover him before it went completely south."

"You saved his life?"

"If you look around you'll find three helpful tribesman, all of whom were waiting—concealed—to aid your friend." Flame shrugged. "I don't think he would have survived that help."

Flame finished loading the unconscious cameraman into the vehicle and climbed into the driver's seat. "Now let's get out of here before more of the peaceful Sunni show up."

He slammed the car into gear and gave it enough gas to climb into the open before turning east...

***

Dana gave a single fist-pump as the dot on her laptop began to move. *He did it!* She didn't for a moment believe that Flame would drive away without the people he'd gone in looking for, therefore... *He got them.* She knew it deep inside. *He's got them!*

She knew she should contact the German network that was employing them to let them know as well but decided that could wait until Flame regained contact with her.

Come on big guy! She turned the volume on her receiver up. *Let me know you're all right!*

***

Flame was trying. He'd turned the radio back on as soon as he cleared the wadi and got the Rover moving along a hard-packed trail that he knew led to a real, concrete, road.

So far, however, he was getting nothing but static and the occasional burst of Arabic chatter with a military cadence.

"They are talking about sending in an air strike," Karin, who had been sitting beside him in silence, suddenly put in.

"You speak Arabic?"

"A little." She shrugged at his glance. "It helps with my work."

"Rest of the crew as well?"

"I speak it fairly fluently," Dieter put in from the back seat. "And I would like to move up front with you two. This one," he pointed at Eric still lying senseless on the seat, "stinks!"

The cameraman had lost sphincter control when he believed he'd been shot, filling his pants with a combination that, as time passed, was becoming quite pungent.

"There's no room up here," Flame grinned. "Pull his pants off and toss them out—it'd smell better if you did."

"Do not do that." Karin turned to her technician. "He would never forgive us for the humiliation."

Dieter thought about it for a moment, then shrugged. "You're right." He leaned forward. "And as you're being so thoughtful..." A grin lit his face. "Switch seats with me!"

"Dieter!"

Flame shut his eyes for a moment. *It's like travelling with a bunch of kids!* He thought about all the trips he'd taken with his SEAL brothers, how quiet they'd been, how focused...

Forget about that! He scolded himself. *That's over.* He glanced at the friendly argument between the reporter and her tech. *This is the kind of thing I'm going to be doing from now on.* He shook his head. *God help me!*

He saw the concrete ribbon of a real road ahead and pushed down on the gas. He couldn't get to Baghdad fast enough.

Chapter 14

At that same moment, half a world away, a quartet of large and well-armed Mexicans rolled down a similarly ill-kept roadway.

"How much further?" Mapache asked his driver.

"Two, maybe two and a half hours."

"Wake me when we're an hour out." The big Mexican folded his arms across his chest and yawned. "We can make final plans then."

The driver nodded, veering to the left to avoid a pothole. He knew that his boss wouldn't be happy if he disturbed him now.

He kept his eyes on the road, concentrating on getting the smoothest ride possible...

Two hours later, he slid to a stop in the parking lot of Doctor's Hospital in downtown Monterrey. "We are here, *jefe*."

"You made good time." Mapache glanced at his rather ostentatious Rolex. "Very good time."

"Thank you."

"There is a Hotel Four Points Sheraton about a block from here." The big man opened the door, motioned for the two in the back seat to follow. "Drive there and reserve rooms for the four of us." Mapache grinned. "Try to get a suite for me."

"*Si, jefe.*"

"When you are done, come back to pick us up." He turned toward the hospital entrance. "We should be finished by then."

Chapter 15

"Thank you so much, Flame." Karin gave him a hug and a quick kiss on the cheek as she slipped a card with her phone number into his hand. "Thank you for all you have done."

Flame had finally managed to contact Dana just before reaching Kabala. She told him to deliver the Germans directly to their embassy—she would meet him there.

"Nice job," Dieter slapped him on the back, his hands full of gear. "I didn't think we were gonna get out of there."

Flame nodded—and watched the two head for the embassy gate.

"I hope you do not think that I will thank you." Flame hid a smile as Eric picked up the last of the gear. He had tried, after recovering, to clean himself up—to little avail. "You are a killer—not a savior."

"No sweat," Flame let the grin spread across his face. "Although I do think you should offer to clean up the back seat of the Rover." He pinched his nose. "It stinks back there!"

Eric snorted and turned to the embassy gate, not once looking back at the man who saved his life.

"I thought I told you not to start any wars." Dana had watched the entire thing from the roadside. "That man really doesn't like you."

"The others do," he turned to his partner. "And two out of three ain't bad." He raised an eyebrow. "We get paid?"

"With a bonus." She slapped him on the shoulder. "You did good, big guy!"

"Thanks." He smiled and looked down at his dusty jacket and pants. "Can I go get a shower now?"

"Seems like a good idea." She turned toward the car.

"Don't sit in the back." Flame shook his head. "I'm gonna have to hose it out before I give it back to Scud."

Dana laughed and climbed into the passenger seat, ready for whatever came next.

***

Mapache indicated that his men should take a seat in the Hospital's waiting room, and then approached the main desk. "I am here to see Dr. Farber. Would you tell him I am here?" he asked the pleasant-looking young woman seated there.

"Do you have an appointment?" The woman gave the rather unkempt figure of Mapache a quick glance. "And may I ask what this is about?"

"Tell him that I have some very serious business to conduct with him. Business that must be…" Mapache gave a smile that showed bad teeth thickly stained with nicotine. "Quite private."

She recoiled a little—then regained her composure. "I will let him know you are here." She nodded toward the waiting room. "If you will have a seat over there…"

Mapache watched her speak into a house phone before strolling back to the waiting room. Farber had no idea who he was but, if his reputation was correct, he would feel obligated to see what Mapache wanted of him and would not keep him waiting too long.

He didn't. Mapache heard the ring of the elevator that heralded the appearance of Dr. Farber less than five minutes later.

"Mr. Mapache!" The doctor was a smallish man, nervous, high-strung and possessed of a particularly annoying voice that held the touch of an unfamiliar accent. "What can I do for you?"

"This is not for all ears, Dr. Farber." Mapache glanced around the waiting room which held ten or twenty patients and their families. "Perhaps we could speak in your office?"

"Of course," Farber stepped back and motioned for the big man to precede him. "This way, please."

A quick trip in the elevator took them to the fourth floor where the resident physicians and hospital administrators had their offices. Mapache followed Farber down a long hall to the corner suite—as hospital administrator the doctor had the biggest office in the building, and the best view.

"Now, Mr. Mapache." Farber motioned to a comfortable chair. "Perhaps you can tell me what you have come here for?"

Mapache waited for the doctor to step past him, then closed the door and set the lock. He took a moment to check Farber's desk, making sure that there were no recording devices or other security systems.

Satisfied, he took the chair and looked his host directly in the eye. "I am told that your hospital is the only one in Northern Mexico that can quickly order Cobalt-60."

"That is true," Farber was confused. "But you are not an oncologist—I know all such specialists in this area." He leaned forward, eyes alert. "What do you want with such a dangerous substance?"

"It is not important why I need the Cobalt-60." Mapache leaned back in his chair. "What is important is the fact that I can give this hospital quite a large grant for the repairs and upgrades you need." His eyes held those of the doctor. "And I will give you such a grant *if* you give me what *I* need."

"But…"

"Dr. Farber…" Mapache leaned forward, eyes suddenly hard. "I need a quantity of Cobalt-60." He stood up and leaned on the other man's desk. "And I need it now."

Chapter 16

Two days later, Flame and Dana were back in the DC area. They took a cab from the airport to their new office on the tenth floor of an office building in Crystal City—right across the Potomac from the Capital and just a few blocks from the Pentagon.

"You did a good job back there, Flame." Dana dumped her travel bag on the floor next to her desk and took out her laptop. "I was worried about sending you out there without back-up."

"I won't lie," Flame dropped his own, somewhat heavier, bag alongside hers. "It would have been nice to have another set of eyes and ears when I was operating near Tikrit—but it was good for me to find out that I could still cut it."

"Literally?" Dana had seen his combat knife when he took it out to clean and sharpen it upon their return to the hotel.

"You don't really need to know that." He shrugged. "Besides, it was all part of the service." He flopped down on the leather sofa that was the only nod to luxury the office boasted. "Anything waiting for us?"

Dana had hooked the laptop into the office's secure server and was scanning the emails that had backed up while they were in flight. "Couple of possibles." She stopped on one missive, leaned forward to read it more carefully. "This might be interesting." She turned toward Flame. "Coptic girl from Egypt is coming here for a UN conference of some kind. Says there's a *fatwah* on the Coptic people and that the Muslims are trying to kill them all." Dana shook her head sadly. "Ethnic cleansing in a big way—and the world is ignoring it." She looked at Flame. "Interested?"

"Where's the money coming from?" He shook his open palm at her look. "I'm not greedy—but we've got to stay in business, don't we?"

"I guess we do." Dana returned to the laptop and scrolled down. "Money comes from the US Department of State." She smiled. "They don't want to be responsible for her—but they know they'll take the heat if she gets killed in the middle of New York."

"Money from the ass-lickers in State, eh?"

"Who better to take it from?"

"Okay." Flame nodded. "Take the job—but make it part of the deal that we get a Federal firearms license and carry permit." He saw her confused look. "I'm going to have to be heeled and New York has some really shitty gun laws."

"Oh," Dana bit her bottom lip. "I didn't think of that." She turned to the computer. "I'll get right on it." She glanced at him. "Where will you be?"

"Right here." Flame yawned and stretched out on the sofa. "Taking a nap."

***

Flame found himself back in that same, vast, dark space. By what was now long habit, he pushed the night vision goggles over his eyes and switched the system on.

The world turned green and white.

It's the dream again. He saw the walls towering around him—and the now-familiar door that he knew led to absolute darkness a few yards in front of him. *I thought I beat this.* He rubbed his chin with his hand, and was unsurprised when he felt the sweat and the start of a beard. *Just like the real mission.* He shook his head. *The last mission...*

The mission where his life as a SEAL ended.

Re-Pete should be here any moment... Flame looked to his right, waiting for the motion that would always signaled his friend's move into position.

It didn't come. Instead there was a whisper of sound to his left. Flame rotated in that direction, rifle ready—although he knew that he wouldn't need it.

Manny hurried past the box that sheltered Flame, a big smile on his face. "There's somebody out there, bro!" He pointed to the door and the darkness that lay beyond. "I can smell him!" He raised an eyebrow. "Can't you?"

Flame took a breath, caught a whiff of cigarette smoke. *Did I miss that before? Is that why that bastard took me by surprise?* He didn't know—he had no mission memories at all from the time he went through the door. *Did I screw the pooch that badly?*

Before he could decide, Manny launched himself through the door, rifle searching for a target.

Flame followed right behind him, eager to find out what would happen. He flattened himself against the door frame, readied his weapon...

"Flame!" The voice echoed in his ears. *It's Manny!* Flame bit his lip, prepared to jump through the door. *I'm coming...*

And then the big room was gone, replaced by the brightly lit office he and Dana had hired.

And he was face-to-face with his petite blonde partner

"The dream again?" she asked.

"You know about it?" Flame sat up on the sofa, rubbing at his forehead.

"I know all about you."

"Then you should never have chosen me to be your partner." Flame looked into her eyes. "I'm psycho—I have dreams about dead people." He shook his head. "How can you trust me?"

"Flame." Dana pulled her chair and sat so she was facing him. "Did you dream while we were in the sandbox?"

"No."

"So you only dream when you're in the world, right?"

"So far, but…"

"But me no buts." Dana's voice was hard. "You did a good job in Iraq—a job that I don't think any other one man could have done—and you did it without freaking out or having any psychic breaks that might have jeopardized the mission." Her eyes held his. "Right?"

"Wrong." Flame dropped his eyes, avoiding her gaze. "I saw something back in that wadi—a hallucination…"

"Tell me about it."

"It was Manny. He stopped me, cued me in to the smell of cigarette smoke. I found the third hadji because of him."

"But Manny wasn't really there—you know that, you knew it then." She touched his chin gently, pulled it up so she was facing him again. "You smelled the smoke—and for whatever reason, your brain chose to use Manny's image to realize it."

"Get someone else, Dana." Flame shook his head. "I'm sure to let you down."

"Fuck that!" Her face went hard. "And fuck your damn dream. You're a good man—and I trust you to do the job." She pushed her chair away. "Besides, there's no time to find a replacement. We just took a job. An important job that needs to be done…"

***

Raphael Mapache was awakened by Felipe, one of his men. "*Federales* and soldiers are surrounding the hotel." The rail thin man nodded toward the window. "I think they are after you."

"Do nothing, my friends," he told his man. "Tell the others to put their weapons away and open the door." The weathered gangster pulled on his pants. "Our doctor friend has made a large mistake. One he will come to regret."

As Felipe rushed into the other rooms of the suite to relay his boss's orders, Mapache touched a button on his cell phone and, as soon as there was an answer, relayed a series of instructions.

He had just finished when the door burst open and federal police officers rushed in, shotguns and machine pistols at the ready.

"We give up, gentlemen." Mapache showed them his hands. "We will go with you peaceably." He smiled a broken-toothed smile. "I am, in fact, looking forward to having a little talk with your superior officer."

Chapter 17

Flame decided to take a nice long run before turning in. He hoped that if he could run far enough, the fatigue might make his sleep dreamless.

He feared that he would never be able to tire himself enough for that to happen.

Why am I having these dreams? he asked himself as he wound his way along the George Washington Memorial Parkway—the road that made its serpentine way from Crystal City to the Iwo Jima Memorial. *Is there something wrong with me?* He ran past a handful of joggers all of whom were maintaining a 'steady' pace that any SEAL would sneer at. *Am I psychotic?*

Flame had been reassured when the dreams stopped after his team-up with Dana. He'd slept well for more than a week before the trip back to Iraq. Even in the sandbox with all those reminders of past missions around him he'd been dream free.

And then this afternoon it all comes back! He wondered if Dana's explanation was true, that somehow his subconscious mind was using dreams and hallucinations to pass information to his waking mind. It certainly did *something* like that in that

Wadi. *I would have run right past that hadji if Manny hadn't tipped me off to the odor of tobacco.*

But had it been Manny? After all, the big Jewish SEAL was dead. Maybe Flame's mind had simply supplied the information in a form that he could relate and react to.

But that's crazy, he told himself. *I would have to be insane for that to be true!*

He ran past another knot of joggers near the Arlington Memorial Bridge.

Maybe I am. He shook his head. *The question is, can I still function? Can I still get the job done?*

Dana thought he could. She had told him so.

Am I going to let her down like I did Re-Pete and the others? He bit into his lower lip and remembered something Chilli had said before the UBL raid. 'We're all crazy for doing this kind of work,' he had told the rest of the team. 'But it's a good kind of crazy.'

Flame vowed that he'd make sure he was *always* a 'good kind of crazy.'

Two hours later he returned to the small apartment he rented in Alexandria. Once there he showered, had a light snack, and went to bed.

He didn't have a single dream of any kind.

***

As Dana and Flame slept, an NSA computer registered a Mexican phone call to the known agent of a terrorist group. Such calls were not unusual—many Mexican gangs and drug cartels maintained close contacts with such groups, helping them move people and gear across the border in exchange for drugs from Afghanistan and other countries under Islamist control.

What made this call different was the fact that it came from the office of the chief of police in Monterrey. The computer noted the oddity—as it had been programmed to do—and generated a report that would be added to the morning summaries.

It took no further action—as it had also been programmed to do.

The report was ignored by the analyst responsible for sifting through the morning data and the NSA took no action.

Chapter 18

Flame was in good spirits when he walked into the office the next morning. "Get the things we need for the UN mission?"

"Most of them." She looked at him with just the hint of a question in her eyes. "You're feeling good today."

"No dreams last night." He smiled. "Not one."

"Good to hear."

"You did get the licenses?"

"Federally-issued carry license came through this morning." She handed him a sheaf of papers. "The Federal Firearms License that you'll need for automatic weapons will take a couple of days."

"That's okay." He took the paperwork, and glanced through it. "This covers both of us." He dropped into the couch and looked at his partner. "What kind of handgun do you carry?"

"I don't have one." Dana's eyes widened with surprise. "I've never fired a handgun of any kind."

"I thought your dad…"

"My father doesn't matter. My mother hated guns." She looked at him. "Wouldn't let one in the house." She sighed. "It's a long story…"

"No time for it now. We have to get a weapon for you and a better one for me." Flame leaned forward, eyes on his partner. "Even if you never use it, it would be good if you had something you could defend yourself with."

"But I don't know how to shoot!"

"We can fix that." Flame made a dismissive gesture with his hand. "I'll teach you how." He tossed the papers onto the desk. "Now, when does this girl we're going to protect arrive— and where?"

"We have three days until she flies into JFK in New York."

"Lots of time." Flame stretched. "Let's take a ride. I know just the man to get us both hooked up."

An hour later, Dana's little Volvo pulled into the gravel parking lot of a rather large brick building. A pair of nineteenth century cannons guarded the doorway.

"It's called 'The Museum of Historical Arms,'" Flame popped out and headed for the door. "But it's not really a museum."

"What is it?"

"The best gun shop on the East Coast," Flame grinned. "And it's run by an old friend of mine." He pushed a button on the doorframe and stared at the rather obvious surveillance camera set into the brick wall. "It's me, you son of a bitch! Open up!" There was a loud *buzz* and he pushed the door open, holding it for Dana to pass through. "You'll like him—I promise."

The interior of the store was a jumble of interlocking walls and showcases, each of them filled with guns of every type and make imaginable.

"Look!" Flame pointed to an odd-looking rifle on the wall. "That's a Istiglal Anti-Material Rifle!" He shook his head. "It's from Azerbaijan. I didn't think there were any in this country."

"Only this one." A slender, light-skinned black man of medium height approached them from the end of the room. "We have a Turkish Kalekalip 12.7mm AMR, too."

"Garland Bremby!" Flame grabbed the man by the shoulders and half-lifted him off his feet. "It's good to see you, man!"

"Nice to see you too," Bremby smiled. "Now could you put me back down?"

"Sorry." Flame carefully set the other man down on what Dana could now see were artificial legs. "Bramble here was in the 10th Mountain Division back in Afghanistan. They were supporting us on a mission a couple of years back..."

"My platoon got careless," Bremby added. "Tripped an IED cluster." He tapped on his thigh, smiling at the sound it made. "I was lucky to get out alive."

"And now you sell guns?" Dana looked around. "Where do you get so many foreign weapons?"

"My brother is a quartermaster. His unit captured one of Saddam's palaces while he was in the sandbox—the bastard's gun collection was inside." Bremby grinned. "He liberated it— sent it back here."

"How did he get away with that?" Dana was puzzled— captured weapons like this were supposed to go through a special screening process.

"My other brother was Brigade Commander," Bremby's grin widened. "He handled the paperwork."

"Nepotism the way it should be." Flame clapped his friend on the shoulder. "Ain't that true."

"It is—but you didn't come all the way down here to talk about the collection," Bremby's face turned serious. "What do you need?"

"I need a handgun for the lady." Flame nodded toward Dana. "And some range time to begin training her in just how to use it."

"Should be no problem," Bremby looked Dana over—in a very professional sort of way. "She's too light to handle a large caliber pistol..." He turned to his right, walked between showcases. "I wouldn't recommend a revolver either—double action trigger pull is a bitch."

He stopped in front of one of the cases, pulled out a box. "This here is the new Smith & Wesson M&P Shield." He held up a stubby automatic. "It measures less than an inch from side to side and has an overall length just a hair over six inches. Only weighs about nineteen ounces unloaded." He offered it to Dana. "See what you think."

She picked it up, weighed it in her hand. "It's really light."

"This one is the 9mm—they make it in twenty-five caliber as well but," he glanced at Flame, "there's an old SEAL saying that goes..."

"Never use a lightweight cartridge on a heavyweight opponent." Flame nodded and took the gun from her hand. "Let's get you started out right—the first thing you do when you take a handgun from someone else is..." He ejected the magazine and pulled back the slide. "Make sure it is not loaded." He clicked the magazine back into place and handed the gun back. "You saw how I did that—do the same thing."

Dana nodded, took a moment to locate the magazine release and then matched Flame's motions.

"Good." Flame nodded then turned to Bremby. "Still got a range here?"

"Out back." He reached back into the case, took out a couple of boxes of cartridges. "You'll need these—this particular pistol is chambered for 9mm although I could special order one in 40 caliber."

"Too big for her."

"I agree." Bremby made a motion with his hand. "Shall we adjourn to the range?"

* * *

Dana had never been read in on firearms during her time in the CIA. She was an analyst and analysts did *not* go into the field.

The NSA had felt the same way—which made this the first time she had actually held an honest-to-god pistol in her hand.

Flame had carefully walked her through the basics— how to load the magazine, how to insert, how to seat a round in the chamber. He was a surprisingly good teacher with what seemed to be endless patience. He didn't let her actually point the gun—*excuse me, pistol!* (he insisted on that, too)—at a target until he was satisfied she understood all the safety rules that went with shooting.

Finally, that moment came and he told her to face the target.

"Handguns don't have a huge amount of range," he said as he attached a paper target with the silhouette of a man on it to a metal clasp attached to an overhead rope, then pulled on the rope to move the target downrange.

He stopped when it was about twenty feet away.

"If you can hit at this range, you'll be more than able to defend yourself in situations where a pistol can actually help." He nodded at the target. "I showed you how to use the sights— go ahead and fire three rounds. I want to see what sort of grouping you can manage."

Dana raised the gun, cradling it in two hands as he had taught her, allowing the sights to slowly come to rest on the center of the target's mass. *Not the head*, he had taught her that too. *Go for center mass—better chance of putting the target down.*

She squeezed lightly on the trigger, squinting slightly in anticipation of what was to come...

Even so, she was surprised when the weapon barked, *WHANG!* and jumped in her hand. She fought the urge to close her eyes, resighted on the target and...

WHANG! The second shot didn't shake her as much as the first. This time it only took a long second to make sure her aim was true, then...

WHANG! The third round went downrange.

"Good," Flame was behind her, speaking into her ear. "Now eject the magazine..."

She did so without looking for the button.

"And clear the chamber."

She pulled the slide back, and allowed the live round to fall onto the rest under her hands.

"Now put the weapon down..."

She laid it on the others next to the magazine and box of ammo.

"And let's see what kind of shot you are." Flame pulled on the rope again, this time pulling the target back toward them.

How did I do? She was sure she'd sighted properly. *Did I get anxious and jerk on the trigger?* She feared she might have done that with the third shot.

The target was close now, curled away from her due to its movement.

"Not bad," Flame looked that paper over as it dropped down in front of him. "Not bad at all."

All three holes were in center mass, separated by less than two inches of space.

"You're a natural, partner." Flame smiled at her. "Now," he clipped another target into place, pushed it downrange, "let's see what you can do with a whole clip..."

***

They spent the rest of the afternoon at the gun range where they burned through nearly six boxes of cartridges. When they were done, Dana's hand was sore and she had three long scratches where the slide of her pistol had cut into her skin.

Flame warned me about that, she told herself as she washed the cuts off. *He said that if I didn't grip the pistol right it would 'bite' me.* She grinned. *I guess I got bitten!*

In more ways than one. Dana had thoroughly enjoyed firing the pistol—and had, by the time they quit, become a reasonably decent shot. She was confident that she could hit a target if it wasn't more than twenty or thirty feet away from her and knew that, with more practice, she'd be able to do damage from further away.

"Done cleaning up?"

Dana emerged from the bathroom to find Flame and Bremby waiting for her.

"We figure it's time to go and get some food," Flame smiled. "But first..." He held up a belt holster. "Try this on."

Dana took the lightweight bit of leather in her hand. "Where does it go?"

"Slip your belt through the loop, put it where you can conceal it with a jacket or open blouse."

Dana did as he directed, finally deciding that it was best right at the small of her back.

"That looks fine," Flame held out the little Smith & Wesson. "Now put this in it."

Dana saw the twinkle in her partner's eyes as he handed her the pistol. *This is a test*, she realized. *One I think I can pass easily enough...*

She popped the magazine out of the weapon, pulled the slide back...

"I think you told me that, in your terms, an empty pistol 'ain't worth shit.'" She looked into Flame's eyes. "Did I misunderstand?"

"Nope." The big man smiled and produced another magazine—this one fully loaded. "Try this on for size."

Dana tapped the new magazine against the counter hand to make sure the bullets were properly seated, then slipped the new magazine into the pistol, clicked the grip safety to 'ON' and jacked a round into the chamber. Satisfied, she slipped the weapon into her new holster, testing the feel of it.

It's good, she nodded to herself. *I can reach it with no problems and it should be easy to conceal.* She looked at Flame. "Time for dinner?"

"One last thing." Bremby produced a soft-looking leather handbag. "This is a Coronado Leather Hollister Soft Hobo conceal carry purse," he smiled. "Big name, I know—but it will let you carry your pistol when you can't conceal a holster." He opened a hard-to-see pouch at the front. "It goes in here—safe and easy to access."

"This looks expensive." Dana took the purse from him, checking out the assortment of zipper openings and pouches it offered. "I don't know…"

"It's on the house." Bremby put his arm on Flame's shoulder. "I owe this man way more than that." He smiled at Dana. "Carry it in good health—and watch my man's back."

"I will." Dana smiled and touched Bremby on the arm. "I promise I will." Her smile widened. "Now can we go to dinner? I'm hungry!"

The two men laughed and headed for the door.

Chapter 19

Dr. Farber shivered as he locked his office door. He knew he'd done the right thing in alerting the federal police to Mapache's request but, as someone who'd lived in Monterrey for many years, knew that it was possible the evil-looking man would be able to buy his way out of custody.

And if he did...

I've got to get out of here, Farber told himself. *Get across the border. Stay with my cousins, while Karin looks into this thing. She'll be able to tell me what is best for me to do!*

He had parked his car away from his usual spot, afraid to advertise the fact that he was still in the hospital. Now he hurried through the front door passing a dozing security guard. *Kurt and Shirley are expecting me tonight.* He touched the remote device on his keychain, and heard the chirping sound that accompanied the unlocking of the car doors. *I only have to cross the border and I will be safe.* He climbed into the car; inserted his key. *An hour at most—then I can rest...*

Nearly a pound of C-4, concealed under his seat, detonated as his key completed a circuit.

They didn't find a piece of him big enough to bury.

***

Two days later, just after midday, Flame and Dana were in the International Arrivals Terminal at Kennedy Airport. They had been met by a State Department official who had come to help the girl through customs—and to brief them on the proper way to handle their assignment.

Flame ignored him, as did Dana—although she managed to look interested in whatever the man said.

Smart girl, he nodded to himself. *Let him talk himself out—he does his job and we don't have to deal with any of his oh-so-correct superiors.*

Flame knew it really didn't matter what the man had to say. He and Dana were going to handle this *their* way. *All he has to do is get the girl through customs,* he glanced at the flight information board. *And we can all be on our way.*

The girl had avoided Cairo airport, fearing she'd be recognized there. Instead, she'd made her way to Alexandria International and flown from there via Turkish Airlines to London, where she caught a British Airways flight to JFK.

That flight had touched down a few minutes earlier.

Flame nudged Dana and nodded toward the board. "Flight's here."

"Is it?" Their State Department contact turned his attention to the monitor. "Well then…" He squared his

shoulders—which, in his case, made them sort of triangular—
and marched toward the door into customs, his ID and
paperwork in hand. "I'll have her out to you in a jiffy," he told
them over his shoulder.

"Did he say anything important?" Flame asked, his eyes
scanning the faces around him for any that appeared suspicious.

As this was New York, many of them looked quite
suspicious indeed!

"Nothing we didn't know." Dana shook her head and
pulled out her tablet—she wanted to see if there was any chatter
on the local server that might point to trouble. "He has an
itinerary for the girl—he'll hand it over when he hands her
over."

Flame nodded—and settled down to wait. Even with a
flunkie from State to grease the skids, customs and immigration
was going to take a while.

It did. Nearly thirty minutes passed before Samira Potros
came up the ramp with the flunkie from State trotting along
beside her.

Is that her? Flame couldn't help but stare at his new
charge. She was not at all what he'd been expecting.

Samira Potros was young—perhaps twenty years of age.
She was short—two inches shorter than Dana who was barely
five three. And she was beautiful in a classical Egyptian way,
with a long, graceful neck, strong features and a lean body that
promised much. Flame thought she walked like a wild animal,
pacing forward with a grace that few could match.

"She's going to be a handful," Dana whispered into
Flame's ears. "The newspapers are going to go crazy when they
see her."

State had kept her date and place of arrival secret. The
press would be expecting her to arrive just before the UN
Conference, which started in three days. She had flown in early
to avoid publicity.

"You go get her," Flame scanned the crowd. "I'll fall in behind and keep an eye on things—see if I can spot any watchers."

"Right." Dana stepped forward. "Meet you at the cab stand."

Ten minutes later they were in a cab and en route to the Barbizon Plaza Hotel. Flame had told the driver to take the Belt Parkway rather than head for the Long Island Expressway—the traffic would be lighter and he would have a choice of ways to cross into Manhattan.

Samira seemed enchanted by the whole trip. She marveled at the packed apartment buildings and houses of Brooklyn and gasped aloud when the towers of New York City came into view.

Her excitement convinced Flame to instruct the driver to go over the Brooklyn Bridge—it gave her an excellent view of the city and a glimpse of the Statue of Liberty, which she stared at until it was obscured by the bridge supports.

Once they had reached the other side, they headed up Third Avenue and followed it all the way to 58th Street where they turned west heading for the south side of Central Park and their hotel.

"The traffic here is not as heavy as Cairo," the girl told Dana. "And it is far more orderly."

"You should see it at six in the evening," Flame put in over his shoulder. "It's much heavier then!"

"Do not all the people take the underground train?"

"Some do." Flame shrugged and watched the cabbie hit the horn to dissuade a pedestrian from crossing in front of him. "Many do not."

"May I take a ride on the train?"

"Sure," he said as they avoided a second taxi, which tried to pass on the inside. "We'll talk about your itinerary when we get to the hotel."

"I want to see so many things!" She pressed her nose against the tinted glass of the back window. "The Central Park, the Empire State Building…"

"Make a list." Flame could see the hotel a block ahead. "And we'll discuss it at lunch—after you get a little rest."

"I could not sleep now!" She turned to Dana. "There is so much to do! And I have not much time."

Flame saw his partner's face, frozen in a smile, in his rearview mirror. *Dana's right,* he thought. *This one really is going to be a handful!*

He thought about how they were going to handle that as they cut off another car and turned into the entrance to the hotel.

***

I wish she had gone to sleep, Dana told herself as she accompanied Samira to the first place she 'could not wait' to see. *I could use the rest.*

Although she had lost sight of him, Dana knew that Flame was somewhere nearby, eyes on the crowd, ready to move if he saw anyone suspicious. *I wish I knew how he disappeared so easily.* She smiled. *He's taller than everyone here and has that mop of red hair yet*—she glanced over the crowded street—*I can't see him!*

They had walked to Fifth Avenue and then right toward Times Square. Samira stared at the goods in the various shop windows as they went, eyes widening at the opulence that was everywhere.

"Is the whole country like this?" she asked. "Are all Americans so rich?"

"Most wish they were," Dana smiled gently. "But few can afford to shop on this street."

"So only the rich live in New York—much like the best parts of Cairo."

"Not like Cairo—the rich and the middle class both live in this city, often on the same block." They stopped as a light turned red. "These are the high priced shops," she smiled. "They sell mostly to tourists from other parts of the country and other lands." Dana shrugged. "Later, if you want, I'll show you the quiet parts of the city where everyone else shops."

"That would be wonderful." Samira smiled. "But can we go back to Central Park now?"

"It's back near our hotel."

"I want to see the 'Strawberry Fields.'"

"It's a bit of a hike."

"I like to walk."

Dana sighed—and crossed the street with her charge, reversing direction. Strawberry Fields was, after all, only twenty or twenty-five blocks uptown…

***

Flame was not as good at camouflaging himself as Dana thought. He had followed her out of the hotel and down the street all the way to Fifth Avenue. At that point he realized that someone was following *him*.

That woman. He glanced at a window where he saw a distorted and very dirty reflection of the tall and athletic figure behind him. *She's been back there since I left the hotel.* It seemed impossible that anyone could have found out about Samira so quickly, but... *The State Department is involved in this,* he told himself. *Lots of Arab lovers there—any of them could have leaked the girl's info...*

Flame shook his head. *I'll worry about the leak later.* For now, he saw Dana turn downtown and came up with a quick plan. When he reached the corner of Fifth Avenue, he turned the opposite way—uptown toward the park—and began looking for a spot where he could find out just what the woman following him had in mind...

That spot appeared soon enough. There was construction being done on what he remembered as FAO Schwartz, the famous New York toy shop. The builders had erected a tunnel-like structure to protect pedestrians from falling debris.

Flame headed for that structure.

Once inside and out of sight, he hurried to the far end and flattened himself against the building just beyond. The edges of the structure prevented anyone inside from seeing him until they were nearly at his side.

Flame waited.

Finally, he saw the dim form of the woman who'd been following him rush through the tunnel and stop just outside, eyes searching the crowd for...

"Flame!" Karin Hachtel started when the big man's hand closed on her shoulders. "I thought it was you!"

"Why are you following me, Karin?" Flame led her away from the crowd. "And how did you find out I was here?"

"I saw you in the hotel." Her eyes sought his as she bit her lower lip. "I...I need your help."

"Again?" Flame had dealt with the media once or twice before. It had never ended well.

"Not that kind of help." She looked around. "Is there somewhere we can talk?"

"Not now." Flame considered the situation. "There's something I'm supposed to be doing right now." He looked into Karin's eyes. "You say you saw me at the hotel?"

She nodded.

"Meet me in the lobby at," he glanced at his watch, "ten tonight—I'll listen to you then."

"But…"

"No buts." He shook his head. "Ten o'clock." He started to turn away, then thought better of it and looked at her once again. "And don't follow me. Understand?"

Karin shook her head, troubled.

"See you later." Flame turned away and headed uptown, moving fast. He had to find Dana quickly—he'd been distracted long enough.

***

Dana was surprised to get a text from Flame asking where she was. She'd assumed he was somewhere nearby—keeping an eye on their ward.*Something must have distracted him,* she thought. *I hope it wasn't a hallucination!*

Samira had been surprised by all the tall buildings that bordered Central Park.

"It's so green!" She'd marveled. "Right in the middle of this huge city and it's still green!"

Dana told her it had been by design—that the men who built New York City planned for this oasis of green to give city dwellers a place of comfort. *I don't know if that's true or not,* Dana thought to herself. *But it's a nice story and it seems to make her happy.*

They had stopped near the Alice statue and taken a quick look at the Central Park Zoo before reaching Strawberry Fields. There, Dana stopped to meet with Flame while Samira walked around and checked out the sights of the wide meadow.

"What held you up?" she asked as the big redhead approached.

"Met a former client." Flame's eyes sought out Samira—found her standing a few feet from a vendor's cart, chatting with a man smoking a cigarette. "Remember Karin—the German reporter?"

"Of course."

"Well, she's staying at our hotel—saw me there." Flame's mouth went taut. "She followed me down the street from the hotel. Took me about a block to notice the tail."

"Not a surprise with all the people on the street."

"Maybe, maybe not." Flame shook his head. "Anyway, I led her away from you and the girl then braced her a few blocks away." His eyes narrowed as he saw the man Samira was with gesture energetically. "Any idea who *that* is?"

Dana followed his gaze. "Haven't seen him before." She shifted her attention to Samira. "She doesn't seem to be bothered. Think we should check him out?"

"I'll keep an eye on him," Flame spared her a quick look. "We don't want to spook the girl, do we?"

"No." Dana shook her head. "But just to be safe, try to find out who he is when she leaves."

"Will do."

"Now, about our German friend…"

"Says she has a problem—one that she needs help with." Flame shrugged. "I told her I was busy right now but that I'd meet up with her at ten in the hotel lobby."

"Want me to come along?"

"No," Flame shook his head. "I'll let you know if we need to get..." He smiled. "Professionally involved."

"Okay by me." Dana's eyes went back to the girl. "I'm going to want to take a long shower when I'm done—I'm not used to all this walking!"

Flame smiled. "You could always take the train." He nodded to the side. "The girl's coming back this way—you go with her, I'll see if I can catch up with her friend." The smoking man had left the vendor's area and was heading down a trail toward the west end of the park. "Where are you heading next?"

"I have no idea."

"Text me when you do—I'll catch up." He headed out in the same direction as the smoking man, smiling at Samira as he passed her.

Chapter 20

I guess I've lost him, Flame thought a few minutes later as he looked across the busy traffic on Central Park West. *He could be anywhere by now.* He watched the endless ribbon of car's taillights on the street in front of him. *I'd better get back to where I can watch the girl.* He pivoted and moved back into the park, hurrying to catch up to his charge.

Wait a minute. He slowed as he reached Strawberry Fields. *That guy was talking to Samira alongside a vendor's cart*; he looked at the handful of carts on one side of the road. *Maybe someone there heard what they were talking about.* He shrugged. *It's worth a try...*

"That man was smoking!"

Flame had used a ten-dollar bill to loosen the man up. *I should have kept it to a single,* he thought as the man went on, voice rising with outrage.

"I told him 'Smoking is illegal in New York!' and do you know what he did?" The man's face had gone red with outrage. "He blew smoke in my face and told me to shut up—he tells me to shut up! In front of my own spot!"

"Did you hear what he said to the girl?"

"I *heard* what he said—but I didn't understand a word of it," the man shrugged. "They weren't speaking in English or Spanish or any of the other languages we normally get here." He looked at Flame. "Arabic, maybe, sounded something like that anyway."

"Thank you for your help, sir." Flame passed the man another ten. "I do appreciate it."

She was speaking to that man in Arabic. Flame thought about that. *Maybe she just heard him say something in that language—he could have been on a phone or something.* She might miss conversing in her own language—it was tough to try to speak to others in a foreign tongue, Flame knew that all too well. But other things were also possible—more sinister things.

Flame hurried to the east side of the park, hurrying to catch up to his partner and the girl. He found them at Columbus Circle where Samira had gone ahead to examine the monument at the edge of the park.

"Couldn't catch up to the guy," he told Dana. "But I did talk to one of the vendors. He said he thought they were speaking in Arabic." He looked at Samira. "Do we know that she's who she says she is?" He looked at Dana. "Who vetted her?"

"The State Department."

"Yeah," Flame's face went sour. "Well, I can't say I'm too crazy about the State Department's judgment these days." He scratched the back of his head. "Did we get a picture?"

"No," Dana pulled her phone out. "I'll see if we can get one." She glanced at Flame as she punched in a message. "You know talking to someone in Arabic doesn't prove anything. It might be perfectly innocent."

"Maybe."

"Maybe we should just ask her who the guy was and why she talked to him." She looked at the girl. "At dinner, maybe…"

"That where you're heading next?"

"She's getting tired—finally," Dana grinned wryly. "So we're heading back to the hotel. I thought we'd eat along the way."

"Carnegie Deli?" Flame suggested. "It's famous and they have a variety of different kinds of food there."

"Sounds like a plan." She raised an eyebrow at Flame. "You coming along?"

"Sure." Flame grinned and followed her across the street. "I could use some food about now."

Samira joined them as they crossed over the street and headed down Broadway. Her smile revealed her fatigue but she still stopped to look in nearly every storefront as they made their way down the street to the deli.

***

"Who did I talk to in the park?" Samira licked a remnant of mustard off the corner of her mouth. "I don't know," she shrugged. "Just some man who said hello."

"He seemed to get a little heated with you." Dana had not taken very long to finish her pastrami sandwich and was considering a piece of cheesecake. "Did you argue?"

"No," Samira took another bite of her roast beef. "We just talked."

"The vendor said you were speaking a foreign language." Flame had also had a pastrami sandwich which, in his case, tasted like roast beef. Afterwards, curious, he had ordered a slice of cheesecake. "He thought it might be French."

"Yes," Samira nodded quickly. "We did speak French for a few moments." She smiled wistfully. "I learned that language before the local school was burned down."

"How many languages do you speak?" That from Dana.

"Four," Samira ticked them off on her fingers. "English, French, Spanish and Latin."

"Not Arabic?" Flame interjected. "I thought that was the official language of Egypt."

"Oh," Samira rocked back a little. "Of course I speak Arabic—I thought you meant only foreign languages."

"So you speak five languages."

"Five," she nodded. "Yes."

"How do you order cheesecake in French?" Dana smiled. "I've decided to get a piece." She motioned for the waiter.

"Pourrions-nous avoir deux morceaux de gâteau au fromage, s'il vous plaît?" Samira came out with when he arrived. "Two pieces of cheesecake, please." She grinned at Dana. "That's how you order cheesecake in French."

Flame nodded and sat back in his chair, sipping his coffee as he wondered if this girl was really who she said she was.

***

They took a cab back to the hotel—both Dana and Samira being too tired, and too full, to walk even the four short blocks. Flame escorted their ward to her room, going inside first to check things out. He found nothing out of the ordinary in sight. *But there's something wrong...* He couldn't quite put his finger on it, but he knew, deep down, that there was something in the room that shouldn't be there.

He shook his head and pushed the feeling away, gesturing for Samira to come in. "Just call us if..." he looked around again, then shook his head, baffled. "Call if you need anything at all."

"Yes, I will." She smiled up at him. "Thank you so much for today." She glanced at the doorway. "Thank Dana for me also."

"I will." He nodded and turned to leave. "Get a good night's sleep," he stopped at the doorway. "If today is any example, tomorrow will be a very long day!"

"I can hardly wait!" Samira followed him to the door. "Goodnight."

"Goodnight," Flame turned away but paused to listen for the two clicks that told him that the door was securely locked. Then and only then did he move down the hallway to Dana's room. As he was about to knock on the door, he realized what had bothered him in the girl's room.

There was a smell! He looked back toward her room. The faint smell of cigarette smoke!

Nodding once, he knocked on his partner's door.

***

"You're sure?" Dana had taken a quick shower and barely had time to pull on the terrycloth bathrobe the hotel provided before opening the door for Flame.

"I'm sure." He was pacing the living-room portion of the suite they shared. "I knew there was something as soon as I stepped inside but I didn't realize what it was until I was almost back here."

"It could have been the maid cleaning up the room."

"Smoking is illegal in New York—inside or out. Her room is not designated for smoking."

"So you think that someone was in her room?"

"I think the man she met in the park was in her room." Flame's voice held a tone of assurance. "I think he's working with her—or vice versa."

"To what end?"

"Too early to tell." He shook his head. "We'll have to be really careful." He turned to Dana. "Did we get a picture yet?"

"No." She shook her head disgustedly. "No answer at all."

"Figures." Flame glanced at his watch. "Well, I think I'll hit the hotel fitness center and lift for a while then shower and meet our German friend at ten."

"You want me to go along?"

"No." Flame shook his head. "You stay close to our girl in case something happens." He opened the door that connected to his own bed and bathroom. "And if you hear from State, let me know right away."

"I will do so." Dana looked at Flame. "Be careful," she smiled wistfully. "I'm not all that sure I can shoot anyone if it comes to that."

"Leave the shooting to me." Flame smiled. "I've had lots of experience." He stepped into his own room and shut the door behind him.

***

The hotel heath center was fairly well equipped and nearly deserted with only one other person—a good-looking stewardess in a well-worn workout suit—there when Flame arrived. The girl, who Flame learned through casual conversation was a stewardess, concentrated on the treadmill, which left the various weight machines free for Flame. He was able to get in a very satisfying workout—and the girl's room number—before he had to rush back upstairs and prepare for his meeting with Karin Hachtel.

She was waiting in the lobby when he arrived.

"Flame." She rose to greet him. "I was afraid you would not come."

"No sweat," he shrugged. "But I don't have very much time. Tell me your problem."

"It is my uncle…" She looked around. "Can we go into the coffee shop? It seems a little more private there."

"Sure." Flame gestured her toward the appropriate side of the lobby. "You're buying."

A few minutes later, with two cups of coffee on the table and the waiter on the other side of the room, Karin began to tell Flame her problem: "I have an uncle in Mexico," she began. "He was born in Argentina," she looked at Flame. "His grandfather was SS—an officer who fled after the war's end."

Flame shrugged.

"My uncle—his name is Axel Farber—is Chief of Medicine at a hospital in Monterrey, Mexico."

"And?"

"Three days ago, he sent me a long email. Before I had a chance to read it, I found out that he was dead." She looked into Flame's eyes. "Killed when his car exploded."

"Exploded?"

"The Mexican police say it was just an unfortunate accident." Karin shook her head. "But the car was completely destroyed." She held his eyes. "I have seen such damage many times before."

"A bomb in the car."

"Yes."

"And the email?"

"It's incomplete—there was some sort of problem in the Mexican router—but what is there is frightening."

"Frightening how?"

"Have you heard anything about the theft of Cobalt-60?"

Flame stroked his chin. "I seem to recall something about a shipment being stolen during a trip from a hospital to a recycling plant." His eyes lit. "That happened in Mexico, didn't it?" He looked at her. "But I thought the police recovered the stolen truck as well as all the Cobalt-60."

"That was the report." She pulled a tablet out of her bag and tapped in a series of commands before turning the screen to face Flame. "But according to other sources, that Cobalt was never completely recovered—and a second shipment disappeared less than a week later."

"I see." He glanced through the articles displayed. "Your uncle put you onto this?"

"My uncle told me that a man named Mapache visited him and asked him to order a quantity of Cobalt-60 from a repository in the US." She looked into Flame's eyes: "He did not trust the man so he called the local police." She shrugged. "He was dead less than thirty-six hours later."

"Have you reported this to anyone?"

"I sent the information to your FBI. They told me…" She looked as if she had sucked on a lemon. "They told me that the Mexican authorities had already recovered the radioactive material and that there was nothing to fear." Her eyes found Flame's. "Nothing to fear!"

"I see." He sat back, ignoring the now-cold coffee. "And what do you want me to do?"

"Look into this. See what you can find out." Her eyes still held his, begging now. "Stop whatever is going to happen." She looked down. "Revenge my uncle."

"I'll go over this with my partner," he told her. "And we'll see what we can do." He lifted her chin. "Understand, there's nothing much we can do until we finish with this UN job."

"But you will look into it?"

"You have my word."

"Thank you, Flame-with-no-last-name. Thank you very much."

***

Flame headed straight for their suite, anxious to see if Dana had gotten an answer from State. He had just passed Samira's room when he came to a full halt.

That's cigarette smoke, he realized. *It's coming from inside Samira's room.* Flame slipped up to the door, put his ear against it. *Can't hear anything inside—certainly no arguments or cries for help.* He wondered what he should do. *Do I break in? See who's in there?*

He shook his head. *Not yet!* He turned and headed for the suite he was sharing with Dana. *Not until I get some back-up!*

Dana still had received no answer from the State Department. She wanted to know what Karin had had to say but Flame cut her off before she could ask: "Get your pistol." He left her gaping at him as he hurried into his own room. "I need you to cover me." He slapped a magazine into the Browning 9mm he'd gotten from Bremby.

"Cover you from what?"

"I don't know." He pulled back the slide; let a round lock into the chamber. "I can smell cigarette smoke just outside Samira's room."

"Shit." Dana stepped into her own bedroom, returned holding her S&W, magazine already in place. "Let's go."

Together, Dana clad in nothing but a terrycloth robe, they stalked down the hallway until they were facing Samira's room.

"Smell it?" Flame whispered. The odor of tobacco was strong in the hallway.

"Yes." Dana held her pistol in both hands, just as she'd been taught. "How do you want to handle this?"

"Like this." Flame motioned her to the side, and then stepped up alongside the girl's door, ready to knock and see what happened.

"Wait!" Dana's hand closed around his. "There's a better way."

"I should have thought of this sooner." Dana led him back to the suite they shared. "Watch the room for a minute," she told him, and turned to rummage in her bag. "Let me know if anyone moves."

"Nothing so far," Flame glanced back at her. "We should really find out if Samira has a visitor."

"We will," Dana produced a black plastic box—about two square inches and one thick. "We'll use this." She stepped past him, and walked to a point opposite the girl's room.

What the hell is she up to? Flame watched as she knelt down and pushed the plastic square against the floorboard. She wriggled it once to make sure it was secure, then stood and headed back to the suite.

Flame noted that her robe had fallen slightly awry— enough to reveal a rather shapely leg—which he immediately moved his eyes away from. *She's my partner,* he told himself. *My partner!*

Dana brushed past him, signaling for him to close the door.

"How're we gonna watch if the door is closed?" he asked.

"With this." She punched a series of commands into her laptop, which a moment later displayed a very clear image of the girl's door. "That was a webcam," she smiled. "I wish I had a white one to match the woodwork," she shrugged. "Next time."

Flame nodded slowly, understanding flooding into his eyes. "The computer will record anyone who enters or leaves the room..."

"And if someone does, they won't know that we know."

"Nice." Flame smiled slowly. "Very nice." He leaned closer. "Anything from State?"

"Nothing at all." Dana leaned back in his chair. "Now, you were going to tell me what our German friend had to say?"

"Oh," Flame nodded. "Yeah, maybe you can get someone to look into it." He sank into one of the easy chairs and began to tell his partner the story of uncle Axel and the Cobalt-60...

***

"I thought the Mexican police found the hijackers of that medical waste truck," Dana remembered the newspaper coverage at the time. "They were supposed to be hospitalized and the Cobalt recovered..."

"Karin says the cops were paid off," Flame shrugged. "That isn't too hard to believe considering it happened in Mexico."

"She says they got another shipment we haven't heard about?"

"And are looking for one more—seriously enough to kill her uncle for trying to turn them in."

"This is way too big for us," Dana turned to her laptop. "It should go to the FBI."

"Karin says she talked to the Feds and they told her not to worry about it." Flame shrugged. "Maybe they already knew and are trying to keep it quiet."

"Or maybe they just don't want to go to the trouble of looking into something that happened on the other side of the border." Dana sucked at her lower lip as she typed something into her computer. "I know how hard it was to get them to co-operate in finding that explosive mini-sub..."

"Know anybody there?" Flame leaned forward. "Anyone we can trust?"

"Maybe." She kept her attention on the keyboard. "I'll certainly pass the info along to the proper people."

"And if they don't respond?"

"We'll worry about that later." She typed in one more set of commands. "For now, I think it's time we got some rest." She nodded at the computer screen. "We'll know more about the girl and her possible visitor in the morning."

"Okay," Flame stood. "I'm going to go for a run come daybreak—shall I bring back some coffee?"

"And bagels." She smiled. "You can't get New York bagels anywhere else in the world!"

"Coffee and bagels," Flame nodded. "You got it." He stepped to his door—and stopped in mid-stride. "Hey, did you..."

"Already done," she displayed her little S&W in one hand and its magazine in the other. "You're kind of slow tonight."

"Guess I'm tired." Flame went through the door, half-closed it behind him. "Goodnight."

It clicked closed.

Chapter 21

The dream came back that night. Flame once again found himself in the now all-too-familiar confines of the lightless room with the hated door to his front and right.

What now? he asked himself as he pulled the night vision goggles into place. *Do I see Re-Pete or Manny?* He clicked the goggles on and peered at the green and white world that surrounded him, waiting for the noise that would herald the appearance of one of his teammates.

When it came, it wasn't from behind him—nor to the right or left—this time it came from directly ahead of him. From the door.

It's Dana, he realized as he saw the slight figure kneeling alongside the darkness of the door. *And she's naked!*

Dana was, indeed, naked—and armed with nothing more than the webcam he'd seen the night before and a squat object that he somehow knew to be a Geiger counter.

"Come on, Flame!" Dana stood, giving him a full-on view of her small but perfectly shaped breasts. "The Cobalt is in there!" She nodded toward the door. "We've got to get it before it can be used!" She turned toward the door, white flesh glowing green in his goggles. "Follow me!"

And then she was gone—vanished into the darkness beyond that cursed portal. Flame jumped up and ran to follow her—but it was too late. The door closed before he could reach it.

"You have to follow her."

Flame's eyes jerked to his right, locked on the new figure that had appeared there. "Mo?"

"You need that woman, Flame." The redhead was wearing BDU pants and a lightweight t-shirt. "She's your only hope."

"But the door..."

"It's only a door, Flame." Mo leaned closer, smiled. "And all doors can be opened—right?"

Flame nodded. *All doors can be opened—I learned that way back in BUDS.* He took a deep breath, positioned himself and kicked at the door...

It popped open, allowing him to fall through—and down...

He woke when he hit the floor.

***

Damn! Flame sat up on the floor of his hotel room. *What did all that mean?* He glanced at the clock on his bedside table. *Four a.m.* He shook his head. *Might as well get that run in.*

He pushed himself upright, pulled his cross-trainers and running gear out of his overnight bag. *If I take the double-loop around Central Park I can get in ten miles instead of the six or so I had planned.* He nodded slowly. *Yeah, ten miles.* He left the room, headed down the corridor. *It'll help me get my head clear.* He paused in front of Samira's room—the webcam was still where Dana had left it and there was no tobacco smell in the air. *And I think I'm going to need a clear head to figure out what's going on.*

He pushed the elevator button and began to check the settings on his watch—he had a lot of thinking to do.

***

"I think we will need about fifty grams," Mapache said as he took a sip of his drink. "Yes, fifty grams will be enough."

"Fifty grams?" Antonio Calvera, the brand new Administrator of Doctor's Hospital in Monterrey stammered in shock. "It is too much! We do not use that much Cobalt-60 in a year!"

"You will order at least fifty grams." Mapache finished his drink and put it on the edge of the Administrator's desk. "More if you need some for your own use." He leaned back. "Do this and you will be well paid—the hospital will benefit— remember that." He smiled. "Fail and you will meet the same fate as your predecessor." The smile widened. "Remember that, too."

"It will take time…"

"You have five days." Mapache stood up. "I will return at that time."

***

Dana woke to a knock on her door. *What time is it?* She glanced at the lighted clock on the bedside table. *Seven a.m.* She shook her head. *Got to be Flame.* She sat up, rubbed her eyes, and grabbed her robe. *Hope he remembered the bagels.*

He had.

"Still in bed?" Flame put two big cups of coffee and a warm bag of bagels down on the big central table. "What's the matter with you? It's the middle of the day!"

"Maybe for SEAL Team Six." She picked up one of the coffees, took a long swallow and sighed. "But not for me. I got into bed late last night."

"Any word from State on our girl?"

"I haven't checked." She pulled the laptop over, and hit the 'Mail' Icon. "What kind of bagels did you get?"

"All kinds," he passed her the bag. "Plain, onion, salt, poppy seed—you name it." He smiled. "There's lox and cream cheese in there too."

"Have you tasted them? Are they okay?" Dana pulled out a plain bagel. "Thanks, by the way."

"No sweat and yes, I have tasted them." He grinned. "The bagels taste like bagels, praise God, and the cream cheese," he shrugged, "I don't know what it tastes like—but it does taste good."

"Lox?"

"Sorta like clams." He glanced at the laptop. "Anything come in?"

"Nothing from State." She took a bite of the bagel. "Umm—that's good."

"How about the webcam we put in the hall?"

"Let's see…" She brought up another window and Flame could see the doorway into Samira's room.

Always doorways, he thought. *What is it with me and doorways?*

"I'll run it back to see if we got anything." She hit a control, watched as the image began to move backward in time. "There's something…" She stopped the image and Flame could see his own figure looking down at the webcam. "What time was that?" Dana checked the time stamp. "Four-oh-five." She looked at him. "Dreams again?"

"You knew I was planning to get a run in." He opened his own coffee. "What else did you get?"

Dana raised an eyebrow to show her disbelief—then started the image moving backwards again. It slid smoothly back to just after midnight, then…

"There's something." She froze the image. "Who is that?"

"He was in the park." Flame leaned forward to get a better look at the man coming out of Samira's door. "Chatting with Samira in Arabic." He nodded to himself. "I thought that looked wrong."

"I'll take a screen grab and send it out—maybe we can get a name."

"Name or not, it's clear that there's something wrong with the girl." Flame leaned back. "State's got to know something we don't."

"Don't bet on it." Dana finished sending the image to the agencies she thought might help. "State doesn't employ the brightest bulbs in the box—they tend to give jobs to political hacks and sycophants." She took another, bigger, bite of the bagel and settled down to work the net. "Maybe I can find more about Samira Potros on the internet." She looked at Flame. "And maybe you can get a shower—you smell!"

"Back in a few," Flame grabbed another bagel, lathered cream cheese on it, and headed for his bedroom door.

***

Dana was still working at her computer when Flame returned. "Find anything?"

"There doesn't seem to be a single photo of Samira anywhere on the internet." She shook her head. "All the UN releases are print only as are the handful of news reports about her."

"I'll bet you that State doesn't have a photo either," Flame grabbed another bagel and spread cream cheese over it. "That's why they're not answering you."

"Don't you worry about getting fat?" Dana took another bite of her own bagel—the first one he'd handed her.

"I ran ten miles this morning." He took a big bite. "I don't worry too much about gaining weight."

"Maybe I should start running," she said, and pulled the belt of her robe tighter. "After yesterday, I think I could use the exercise."

"Speaking of exercise…" Flame had finally figured out why Dana had been naked in his dream. "Did you have your S&W with you for the whole trip?"

"I didn't…" Dana blushed a little. "I didn't think I'd need it."

"You always carry your weapon while on a mission— and this is definitely a mission!" He looked her in the eye. "Promise me that you will always have your pistol with you from now on."

"I…"

"Promise me!"

"Okay," Dana waved her hand in defeat. "I promise."

"Good." He licked the last of the cream cheese off his fingers. "Now, what's the plan for today?"

Dana pulled out the list of places Samira had asked to visit, pointing to the ones she'd circled for today. "We'll do these today—they're all around midtown. Tomorrow, we go for her biggest wish…"

"The Statue of Liberty." Flame nodded. "She barely took her eyes off it on the trip here."

"She says it was a big deal for her when she was very young. Says she saw it in a magazine and fell in love with it."

"The Statue of Liberty?" Flame frowned. "In Egypt?"

"That's what she says."

"She also says she didn't talk to anyone in Arabic." Flame finished his coffee. "What other lies has she told us?"

"I don't know." Dana took a last bite of her bagel. "I guess we'll find out."

"I guess." Flame glanced at his watch. "Well, as it's almost time for breakfast…"

"Breakfast!" Dana looked at the now half-full bag of bagels. "How can you even think about breakfast?!"

"I'm a growing boy," he grinned at her. "Now go grab a shower and get dressed." His grin widened. "I'm buying."

***

They gave Samira's room a call before they left, informing her that they'd be down in the coffee shop if she wanted to join them.

She did, and arrived at their table only a few moments after they'd been seated.

"Look at all those people!" Their table looked out over Seventh Avenue which, at this time of morning, was quite crowded. "Where are they all going?"

"Most of them work somewhere in this area," Dana put in. "The others are tourists from all over the world."

"I guess I am a tourist as well." An odd smile crossed her face. "Even though I have a job to do here."

"You're a tourist today and tomorrow." Dana's smile matched hers. "Then you have work to do."

"Where will we go today?" She looked from Dana to Flame with bright, inquisitive eyes. "Where in this great city?!"

"First we will go to the top of the Empire State Building," Dana had worked out a route that would allow them to see many of the sights Samira had listed in just one day. "Then to the Freedom Tower…"

"The building that replaced your World Trade Center." Samira nodded. "Yes, I want to see that!"

"From there we will take the subway uptown to the Museum of Natural History."

"The place where the so-called dinosaurs are displayed." Samira nodded quickly.

"So-called?"

"The book tells us how old the Earth is." Samira shrugged. "At least that is what my father taught me." She looked Dana in the eye. "And there are no 'dinosaurs' mentioned anywhere."

"How about Leviathan?" Flame interjected.

"Perhaps," Samira smiled. "It will be interesting to see these 'dinosaur' bones in any case." She turned back to Dana. "What do we do after seeing this museum?"

"I thought we'd get a quick meal somewhere in midtown followed by a Broadway Play." Dana caught the girl's eye. "I got tickets for *The Lion King*."

"Perfect!" The girl's smile lit up the little booth the three of them shared. "And tomorrow, the Statue of Liberty!" She smiled. "It will be the trip of a lifetime!"

The waiter chose that moment to bring their food, which, for Flame and Samira, pretty much ended the conversation.

Dana, nursing a cup of tea, watched as the others wolfed down eggs (Flame said that his tasted like rice), toast, fresh melon, and, in Flame's case, two large cups of coffee. *How does he do it?* she asked herself. *How does he burn off all those calories?*

Then she remembered the kind of things he and his comrades did on a regular basis—and knew the answer to *that* question.

***

Thirty minutes later, the three of them were walking down Seventh Avenue. Dana had suggested a taxi but Samira had told her it was a fine day and she wanted to look at all the wonderful shop windows they would pass along the way.

They reached Herald Square about an hour later and took a few moments to walk through Macy's, Dana kicking herself for not thinking to put it on their itinerary. Soon they were in the lobby of the Empire State Building, Samira marveling at the art deco fixtures that were such a big part of its decoration. Later, on the observation platform 102 stories above Fifth Avenue, Dana and the girl looked out over the city while Flame kept an eye on the people around them.

"It is truly beautiful," Samira said wistfully. "Far more so than Cairo…"

"You can see the park from here," Dana led her to the northern side of the platform and pointed at the green rectangle. "And our hotel right alongside."

"Where is the Statue of Liberty?"

"You should be able to see it from this side." They moved to the south. "There it is," Dana pointed. "Out there in the harbor."

"And we will be there tomorrow?"

"Tomorrow."

"Good." Samira smiled. "I so look forward to that." She stared out over the city. "I can't tell you how important it is to me..."

Dana studied the girl's face as she looked out over the harbor. *Flame's right*, she decided. *She seems genuine enough but there's something there, something deep under the surface...*

She sighed. *We should call in the FBI, hand her over to them.* That, of course, would seriously embarrass the mighty State Department who had brought this girl—no matter what she might turn out to be—into the country. *We'd never get another job from anyone in government*, Dana knew. *We'd be out of business.* She glanced back at the girl's eager face. *Still, it would be the safe thing to do.*

Dana smiled. *I've always done the safe thing—the proper thing. Look where it's gotten me.* She glanced at Flame, saw his eyes flicker over the crowd. *It's time to do things his way—plunge in and take things as they come.* Her face hardened as she touched the pistol in her handbag. *Just make sure you're ready to do whatever's necessary from then on.*

***

The rest of the day went smoothly enough. Samira was unimpressed by the Freedom Tower—the barbed wire-tipped fence around the still-under-construction second building confused her.

"I thought America was a free country," she said. "Why do you have such a barrier around a building that is supposed to represent that freedom?"

Dana tried to explain vandalism and petty theft, comparing what would happen here without the fences to what did happen to the Egyptian pharaohs buried in the Valley of the Kings—but it did no good. Samira left the Tower with a sour taste in her mouth.

One shared by Dana and Flame.

Her spirits quickly returned, however, when they took her to the subway. She was thrilled by the bustle and excitement of the station and amazed by the speed and comfort of the E train as they went uptown.

They changed at 42nd Street, giving the girl a wide-eyed look at a *really* busy station, then took the C train uptown to the American Museum of Natural History where all three of them spent the rest of the day roaming through halls devoted to the history of the people of Earth and the creatures that roamed the Earth before man.

Only once did Samira ask a question that seemed unusual. They were in the Cultural Halls—an area filled with various displays of clothing, weapons and goods that had been part of the museum for more than a hundred years. Samira stopped in front of an exhibit case full of tribal costumes and weapons. "How did they get all the things that are on display here?"

"The museum sent expeditions to all kinds of places in the early part of the twentieth century," Dana told her. "They brought back samples of everything they could find."

"They didn't steal them?"

"I don't think so," Dana was confused by the question. "Why do you ask?"

"No reason," the girl shrugged. "I've been wondering where the big skeletons we saw upstairs really came from." She looked at Dana. "Who made them?"

"Nobody made them." Dana showed a touch of confusion. "They came out of the ground in places like Montana and Utah…"

"But how is that possible? As I told you, there is no record of them in the great books of the world."

"They lived long before humans—millions of years ago."

"If you say so," Samira's mouth turned up in a quirky, disbelieving smile. "Can we look at the gemstones now? I have never seen an emerald or a star sapphire and this book," she held up the museum guide, "says there are examples of both in the Hall of Minerals."

"Of course." Dana led the way out of the Cultural Hall, noting the look Flame threw her and headed through the remainder of the Hall of Human Origins and into the Ross Hall of Meteorites.

"Wait!" Samira stopped and read the plaque at the entrance. "There are meteors—fallen stars—in this hall?"

"That's what it says."

"I would like to see." She walked into the hall. "I have always wanted to see the Haram al-Sharif—but was never able to get there. Perhaps these rocks are similar…"

They spent the next thirty minutes studying the jagged nickel-iron rocks that lined the hall, then another hour looking over the gemstones and carved treasures in the Guggenheim Hall of Minerals.

"These are magnificent." Samira looked over some of the larger stones. "Fit for the emperor of the world." She smiled. "Or a president—whichever."

"I don't know," Dana smiled as she looked over some of the emeralds and jade carvings. "Some of these are a little over the top—don't you think?"

"Perhaps." Samira shrugged and looked at her wristwatch. "I am suddenly very tired. Could we go back to the hotel so I can rest a little before we see *The Lion King*?"

"Sure." Dana stepped closer. "Do you want to go back on the train or would you rather we take a cab?"

"Do you think we might take one of your cabs?" Samira smiled. "I would like that."

"Okay," Dana led them to the side exit and out the 77th Street exit where a cab was pulled up on the access circle. They climbed in and headed back to the hotel.

The cab, Dana soon realized, reeked of cigarette smoke. She glanced at Flame who showed no concern at all although she could see his hand was resting on the butt of his Browning 9mm. She thought of reaching for her own weapon but decided, instead, to examine the cabbie's license mounted on the back window.

Budayl Al Hakam Samaha, Dana memorized the name as the cab moved down Eighth Avenue. *I'll check it when we get to the hotel.* She saw Flame's stiff figure out of the corner of her eye. *If we get to the hotel!*

Samira was oddly quiet throughout the trip, her eyes fixed on the front window of the cab and, perhaps, the mirror mounted above it.

This may be her contact, Dana thought. *He was awfully convenient to the Museum and she decided to leave very quickly once she saw the time.* She shook her head a bit. *Hell, I'm getting paranoid. Cabs are supposed to cruise that area. We just got lucky.*

Lucky or not, she kept her hand near the S&W concealed in the front section of her purse—and breathed a sigh of relief when they pulled into the auto entrance of their hotel.

"Come on, Samira." She helped the younger girl out of the car. "You just have time for a nap before we grab a quick meal and head for the theater." She hustled her ward through the revolving door and into the lobby.

Outside, Flame exited the cab after paying the meter. He made sure to get a good look at the driver.

It was not the cigarette smoking man he had seen in the park.

***

"I am disappointed that you will not join us for *The Lion King*," Samira said over a heaping plate of meatballs and spaghetti. "I always feel so much safer when you are around."

"I'm not much for sitting still," Flame replied, looking down at his own spaghetti that he had found tasted uncomfortably like the mealworms he had eaten during survival training. "Have fun with Dana and I'll take the opportunity to get in a run." He smiled. "I did ten miles this morning and I'd like to do another ten miles tonight."

"You run twenty miles in one day?"

"Sometimes more." Flame nodded. "It helps keep me strong and in good shape."

"I have heard that the Central Park can be dangerous at night."

Flame just smiled.

An hour later, with the girls safely inside the Minskoff Theatre, Flame returned to the hotel and changed into his running gear. He warmed up en route to the park and chose to once again use the double-loop path he'd run this morning.

He'd finished the first loop and was nearly to the reservoir when he heard footsteps behind him.

Haven't seen too many other runners, he thought. *Most don't like to come out this late at night.* He concentrated on the sound of the footsteps.*Whoever that is, he isn't used to running.* Flame nodded to himself. *Which means he isn't a runner, which means...*

He waited until the sounds were directly behind him before, in a carefully-timed move, Flame spun around, muscles loose, ready for whatever action was necessary.

The move surprised the dark-skinned man who had approached to within ten feet. He'd been sure that the redheaded American was concentrating on his running or his music—anything other than his back trail.

No matter, the man thought bringing his knife hand up. *He has no weapon...*

He was wrong, of course. Randall 'Flame' O'Donnell didn't need a weapon—he *was* a weapon.

Unaware of this, the attacker went into action with the ease of long practice. He feinted at the redhead's face then drove the blade toward his midsection...

Guy looks like he's done this before, Flame noted as the man in the dark-colored hoodie, dirty jeans, and worn sneakers snaked his blade forward.*I wonder how many harmless runners he's taken advantage of...*

Flame smiled. *Let's see how he handles someone who can fight back!* He ignored the feint, blocking the knife with a lightning-fast move of his left forearm.

"You know," he said as his attacker backed off for another attack, "I'm not sure just how to handle this."

The man with the knife ignored him, instead coming in with a low attack, designed to slip under Flame's ribs and up into his heart.

"In the sandbox, I'd just make you eat that knife…" Flame slipped away from the attack. "But here…" He shifted his weight and slammed the heel of his hand into the knife man's ribs before dancing away again. "I just don't know what the proper etiquette is …"

"Bastard!" The knife man grabbed his injured side and came forward again, leading with the knife in his right hand.

"I'll give you a chance," Flame easily slid away from a poorly-timed slash—and kicked the back of the dark man's knee. "Tell me who you're working for…" Another strike—this time to the face—the force causing the man's injured knee to buckle. "Tell me that and I'll let you go."

"Who are you, man?!" The dark man pushed back onto his feet. "Why don't you die?" In a lightning fast move, he shifted the knife from his right hand to his left striking, in the same move, at Flame's midsection.

The blade almost made contact.

Almost.

"That was a nice trick," Flame's hand closed around the other man's wrist, stopping the knife thrust cold. "If I had time," he kicked the side of the man's knee, which gave with an audible crack, "I'd let you try it again."

"Ahhhh!" The knife man slumped halfway to the ground, held upright only by Flame's grasp on his wrist.

"Tell me who you're working for." Flame turned the wrist away from him, slammed his elbow into the man's face, breaking his nose. "Tell me!"

"I don't know!" The knife man almost screamed the words. "Really! A guy in a bar—he gave me fifty bucks…"

"What did he look like?" Flame increased the pressure on the man's wrist.

"Dark," the man moaned. "Not black—dark. An Arab, maybe. He was a cabdriver—I'm sure of that." Another moan. "He said to look for a big redheaded guy in the park and take him out. Said it had to be tonight..."

"Thanks," Flame took the knife out of the man's now-limp hand and allowed his erstwhile opponent to sink to the ground. "Next time you think about taking this kind of job," he snapped the knife blade between his hands, "remember what happened to you here."

He gave the man one more hard look, then turned and returned to his run. He still had nearly four miles to cover.

Chapter 22

"Something wrong?" Dana had been just about to check her messages when Flame came into the shared living room.

"I got attacked," he shrugged that off. "No real problem there—guy only had a knife."

"Did you shoot him?"

"Shoot him?" Flame shook his head, "Hell, I just told you that he only had a knife! Besides," he gave her a steady look, "I needed to know who hired him."

"He wasn't just a random mugger?" Dana was really puzzled now. She'd grown up on stories of New York crooks; surely anyone who attacked Flame would have to be one of them.

"Not random." Flame took a long pull on the bottle of water he'd brought with him. "Hired to take out a tall, red-haired man." He pointed at his longish mop of hair. "How many of those do you think were jogging through the park tonight?"

"I see…" Dana sighed. "So who did hire him?"

"Somebody he didn't know—an Arab." He looked into her eyes. "A cabdriver."

"You think it was the man who drove us back yesterday? What was his name," Dana dug into her memory. "Budayl Samaha?"

"You sent his name to your contacts?"

"I did," she reached for her laptop. "I was just about to check messages when you walked in." She booted the machine up, entered a series of passwords...

"Well?"

"Look." She turned the screen so he could see it. "State sent this early this morning." They both looked at the image of Samira Potros smiling back at them. There was no doubt that it was the same girl who was in the room just down the hall.

"So she *is* the girl that State brought in from Egypt." Flame finished the bottle of water. "Doesn't mean that she is what they think she is." He nodded toward the console. "Check out the webcam. See if anyone got into the girl's room while we were gone?"

"Good idea," Dana called up the file, ran the footage back at speed searching for someone, anyone, who might have entered Samira's room.

"The only person who went in," she finally proclaimed. "Was the maid—and look at this," she said, as she turned the screen toward Flame. "Check out the pocket of her apron."

"Looks like a pack of cigarettes." He nodded. "So maybe our girl is just who she says she is and the guy who visited her last night was just a relative—or a friend she didn't want us to know about because she was worried it would make trouble for her."

"Do you believe that?"

"Hell no!" Flame dropped back into his seat. "There's something about her that smells wrong."

"What can we do?"

"Listen," Flame leaned forward. "I'm the sharp end of this team—I take out the bad guys *after* you point them out to me." He shook his head. "I'm not an intel guy—I don't follow leads and work out puzzles."

"Understood." Dana sighed again. "Intelligence is my job—I get it." She leaned back in her chair. "Should we turn her over to the FBI? Have them check her out?"

"And admit we can't handle something as simple as a babysitting job?" He smiled. "Might as well just hang up the 'Out of Business' sign and take the loss."

"So what do we do?"

"We act as if everything is fine—take the girl to the Statue of Liberty as planned." He stood up and stretched. "And we watch every single move she makes."

***

Flame had no dreams on Tuesday night and did not wake up until two minutes before his specified wake-up call. He always woke up before his wake-up call—he had done so since his first day of high school. *Just enough time to get a run in,* he thought as he pulled on his gear. *Five miles should be just about right.*

He headed for the park and the short running path, keeping a careful eye on the people who surrounded him—but he saw no assassins, no muggers with guns or knives. His run was uneventful and pleasant enough—although the day had turned overcast and muggy.

Better get back, he thought checking his watch. *It's time to get some breakfast and head for the Battery.* He had checked ferry times and knew that one headed for Liberty Island every half-hour or so. *Lots of choices—and we have all day,* he knew. *But I'd better get a move on.*

He headed for the hotel, unaware of the dark eyes watching from the taxi stand in Columbus Circle.

***

Samira looked a little pale when Dana met her outside her room—and she noticed that the girl's eyes were puffy—as if she'd been crying.

"Are you all right?" She asked.

"I am fine," Samira forced a smile. "It is only that I have been waiting for this day for so long." She turned away from Dana. "Is it truly time for us to go?"

"We'll have breakfast first." The two of them headed for the elevator. "Flame will meet as in the coffee shop."

"Flame has been running again?"

"He runs every day." Dana shook her head. "I don't know how he can manage it."

"It is his way of coping with the world," Samira's voice had an odd ring to it. "His way of dealing with—what is the word—his mortality." She turned a serious face to Dana. "Everyone has a coping mechanism of some kind," she shrugged. "Or at least I have been taught that such is the case."

"You've been taught well." Dana turned as the elevator door opened and ushered Samira into a car that already held five people. "Most people don't understand such things."

"I understand many things," Samira's voice was oddly disconnected. "Many things."

Dana worried what the girl—so obviously preoccupied—was really thinking.

Flame was right, she told herself. *We're going to have to keep a very careful eye on her today.*

She was glad she'd made sure her pistol was loaded and ready in her special bag. She only hoped she wouldn't have to use it.

Chapter 23

The trip down to the Battery was uneventful. They had, once again, taken the subway, emerging a little way from the docks that held the ferries that would take them to Liberty Island.

"Wall Street is only a short walk that way," Dana pointed uptown. "There's a very old church there, perhaps when we're done at the Statue…"

"I don't think so." Samira shook her head. "My own church in Egypt is more than six hundred years old; I doubt there is an older one in this country." She turned toward the ferries. "And Wall Street is an evil place—one I have no wish to visit."

She looked out over the harbor, her eyes locking on the Statue. "It is this Statue I truly wish to see." She smiled. "The most important thing I will ever see."

Dana almost cancelled the outing right then and there—but a quick glance at Flame told her it would be the wrong thing to do. *We've got to handle this*, she told herself. *We have to* prove *that we can be trusted with important tasks*. She nodded to herself. *It's the only way we can make this security thing work for us!*

Fifteen minutes later, they were on one of the ferries, seventeen minutes from Liberty Island and the Statue.

***

All right, Flame asked himself. *Where is he?*

Simple reasoning said that the girl's handler would have to be on the boat with her. Flame had watched every face as he and the two girls boarded the Ferry but had seen no one that looked like either the cab driver or the smoking man.

Things did get a little crazy just before we pushed off. A school group had arrived less than three minutes before the scheduled departure and three busloads of kids had crowded past Flame and onto the ferry.

At that point anyone could have gotten on without being seen.

I have to keep an eye on the girl, he finally decided. *Whatever they're going to use her for, they have to reach her first.* Flame climbed to the upper deck where Dana had indicated she and the girl were headed, his eyes constantly flicking from side to side, his hand never more than a few inches from the Browning holstered in the small of his back.

Dana and Samira were standing at the forward rail, looking out toward the steadily growing Statue that seemed to be rushing toward them. Dana had a cup of coffee in her hand.

As he watched, the girl whispered something to Dana and turned away. *Where is she going?* Flame kept his eyes on her as she crossed the deck heading for the covered cabin behind him. He followed when she opened the hatch and stepped inside.

I don't see the cabdriver or the smoker. He ran his eyes around the room, assessing those he did see...

And realized that he'd lost sight of Samira.

Shit! He moved sternward, searching for the diminutive form of his charge. *Don't see her anywhere!* He reached the rear of the cabin—where the restrooms were located. *Did she go into the ladies' room?* He pulled out his phone and sent a text to Dana. *Only one way to find out...*

***

Dana hurried back to join Flame. *I never should have let Samira go to the bathroom alone,* she told herself. *I should have gone along—kept my eyes on her.*

She shook her head hard. It was too late to worry about that now—she'd flagellate herself when this was all over.

"What do you have?" she asked as she reached her partner.

"Girl disappeared into the crowd." Flame nodded toward the toilet. "Only place I haven't looked."

"I'll check it out."

"Better hurry." Flame nodded forward. "We'll be docking pretty soon now."

The Ladies room had three stalls. Dana opened two of them, found them empty. The third had a locked door. *What do I do?* Dana hadn't been in this sort of position before. *Should I knock?* She felt the ferry bump into the pilings of the dock. *The hell with it!* She slammed her palm against the door and spoke—loudly: "Who's in there?!"

"Excuse me?" A frightened young voice answered. "I'll be out in a moment!"

It was not Samira's voice.

Dana hurried back into the ferry's cabin. Flame was forward, his eyes on the dock. She hurried to join him.

"Call your contacts in Washington," he spat out. "Make sure Homeland Security knows something's going down here." He glanced at her and grinned. "And make sure they know we're in the middle of it—I don't want to get shot by a guard just because he doesn't know who I am."

"Got it." Dana pulled out her phone. "Where will you be?"

"Out there, on the island." His face went grim. "I've got to find that girl before she does whatever she's been planning to do."

And he was gone.

Who do I call? Dana asked herself. *I can't call State—they'll take too long to realize what's happening.* Then it struck her—there was only one person she *could* call. She punched in a series of numbers, heard one ring, two…

"Hello?"

"Admiral!" Dana exhaled in relief. "I've got a situation here…"

Chapter 24

Flame pushed his way through the crowd on the dock, eyes fixed on the Statue. *She'll head there.* He was sure that was her target. *I've got to cut her off.* He found an opening, got free of the swirl of humanity and sprinted up the rise that led to the Statue.

He had almost reached the main entrance when there was a rustle of noise to his left. He whirled to the side—and winced as something hard smashed against his forehead.

"You will not interfere, pig."

Through a slowly lifting fog, Flame saw a man pointing a pistol into his face. *It's the smoking man,* he realized, suddenly catching the stench of tobacco odor that seemed a part of his very being. *Shit!*

Flame wiped at his forehead and felt the welt forming there. *Why hasn't he fired?* He suddenly knew the answer. *He can't shoot!* Flame saw the crowd at the entrance to the Statue. *If he does, they'll scatter and his whole operation will fail.* Flame looked at the man. *He can't shoot...*

The man brandished his weapon and nodded toward a dark door at the side of the Statue's base. "Rise slowly and walk to that door..."

I haven't had a whole lot of luck with doors recently... Flame's mind was weighing distances and angles. *I think I'll avoid that one.* He nodded to the man as if submitting; put a hand flat on the ground to push himself upright...

And then moved with a speed the other man would not have thought possible. He used the planted hand as a base and swept the smoking man's legs out from under him, grabbing the other's gun hand before he could fire.

"Bastard!" He got a knee under the other's arm, used his grip on the man's arm to lift it up and smash it down—hard.

The man screamed and dropped the gun as his elbow shattered—but recovered quickly enough to claw at Flame's eyes. Flame rolled to one side, maintaining his grip on the gunman's wrist, levering it outwards and grinding the broken bones against one another...

The pain must have been incredible, but the gunman somehow maintained consciousness and kept fighting with every bit of strength he had left.

I don't have time for this, Flame told himself. *The girl could have reached the statue by now.* He released his grip on the man's maimed arm and rolled away and onto his feet. He gave the struggling gunman a cold look—then kicked him between the legs with every bit of strength he could muster.

The man rolled up into a ball as his testicles were smashed flat.

Flame didn't let up. He reached down and grabbed the man's chin with one hand and the top of his head with the other. His planted leg gave him leverage as he pulled and twisted—hard.

There was a loud *SNAP* and the man went limp.

Now to find the girl, Flame picked up the fallen weapon, checked the load and stuck it in his belt. *She'll be heading for the base of the statue...*

***

Dana finished her call and rushed off the ship. Flame was somewhere ahead of her—and so was the girl. She knew it would be at least a few minutes before the word made it down to the guards on the island and she hoped that no one would get trigger happy if Flame was forced to use his handgun.

She reached the end of the pier and looked for her partner. *He'll be somewhere near the statue,* she thought. *Because he knows that's where the girl is headed.* She caught a hint of movement to her left and hurried up the pathway, angling away from the main crowd.

There he is! She saw Flame near the Statue's base, his head moving from side to side, scanning the area around him. *He's looking for the girl!*

She saw him stiffen, lean forward, then move with the liquid grace of a jungle cat.

He's found her. Dana picked up her pace, rushing toward the point he'd been staring at. *I only hope he's in time!*

***

Flame pushed and shoved his way through the edge of the crowd blocking the entrance to the Statue. He thought he knew where Samira would be...

If she has a bomb, the best place to detonate would be at the base of the stairway inside, he thought. *It would damage the structure of the Statue and kill most of the people on the stairs.* He shook his head. *Too many people...* He pushed a young man out of his way; slid in front of a family of four. *I have to stop her!*

Flame finally reached the entrance to the Statue, leaving a wake of yelling, cursing people behind him. Inside, a small mob was gathered in front of the elevator that took visitors to the top of the pedestal.

Flame knew that if he had to use that elevator he'd be too late. *Stairs!* He looked around. *There must be stairs here somewhere!* He saw a door marked 'Employees Only' and pulled it open revealing a narrow set of stairs.

He headed up, two steps at a time, changing directions at every landing, going higher and higher. *Should be just about...*

Another door appeared—Flame halted in front of it, took a moment to breathe, certain that Samira was somewhere beyond. *I don't want to make a lot of noise,* he told himself. *She might detonate before I can do anything.* He nodded to himself and stared at the door—the dark green door. *Always a door.* He shook his head. *Ah well...*

He eased the door open and slipped through, eyes searching for his target.

She wasn't too far away.

There! Flame had emerged in an alcove to one side of the pedestal. To his left was the entryway to the stairs that led visitors up into the Statue proper. Samira was just to the side of that entryway. *She's wearing a bomb vest!* Flame had seen enough of the things to recognize the additions that had been made to Samira's trim form since she disappeared on the boat. *She's got the detonator in her hand.* He could see the plastic and metal thing quite clearly. *It's one of the old Russian ones.* He had come across such things in Afghanistan. It worked without batteries. All that was needed was a squeeze of the trigger—the movement turned a little wheel, which generated a spark that detonated the explosive…

What is she waiting for?

He got the answer a moment later as the elevator bell rang and a large group of tourists spilled out and headed for the stairs.

Shit! He pulled his Browning out of its holster. *She's gonna blow the thing as soon as they get inside the entrance.* He lifted the pistol. *I wish I had a rifle.* He knew that if he could hit her hand, shatter the detonator, he could stop it from going off.

A thought crossed his mind, one that had a fractionally better chance of success than risking a shot. *Can I reach her quickly enough?*

He didn't waste the time it would take the time to calculate the odds; instead he left the alcove and ran as fast as he could right at Samira.

***

Dana reached the entrance to the Statue a little after Flame passed through. There was still a knot of angry people cursing the big man who had pushed and shoved his way past them.

Their cursing redoubled as Dana did the same. She ignored them and forced her way into the base of the Pedestal. There was a crowd waiting for the elevator. *Flame wouldn't have gone that way*, Dana looked around to see how he had gone. *There!* A doorway to her right stood slightly ajar. *That's how he went!*

The door led to a staircase that Dana started to climb as quickly as she could. *Something's about to happen!* She knew that as well as she knew her own name. The only question was— would she get there in time to do something about it.

***

Samira turned toward Flame just before he reached her. *She's gonna blow the device!* Flame threw himself forward. *God help me!* He reached for the triggering device, pushed his fingers between the trigger and the plastic casing...

I got it! He started to slip to the floor. *Gotta hold on!* His left hand was jamming the trigger device, preventing Samira from detonating the bomb vest. Flame's knee touched the ground, giving him just enough leverage to regain his balance...

He looked up just as the knife flashed toward him.

Shit! Flame threw his right wrist up, deflected the blade enough to miss his face. He tried to grab the girl's wrist before she could cut at his left hand—but he was still off balance, giving her the edge. The knife flashed again and Flame winced as it cut the back of his left wrist, just missing the tendons.*Gotta stop this!*

Flame planted his feet firmly on the floor and, in one movement, smashed his right palm into the girl's face. Her nose exploded, blood temporarily blinding Flame as the girl sagged.

He didn't give her a chance to recover. He hit her again, watched her eyes flicker. *One more time.* His elbow swept around, impacting the tender area just below her temple.

Samira Potros, or whoever she was, crumpled into his arms, senseless.

Flame lowered her to the floor, pried her right hand away from the detonator—and noticed that a crowd had gathered around him.

"Get out of here," he yelled. "She's got a bomb!"

He heard gasps, whispered questions.

"I said," he pulled Samira's jacket open, revealing the bomb vest, "get out of here!"

There were cries of fear as the crowd pulled back.

"Get the fuck out of here!" Flame drew his pistol and pointed it at the person closest to him. "Do it!"

It was enough. The crowd streamed backwards, pushing and shoving their way to the elevator and safety.

***

Dana was puffing and fighting for breath as she reached the top of the stairs. *God, I'm out of shape!* She leaned against the doorway and fought to regain her wind. *I've gotta start exercising!* She nodded and turned toward the door, closing her hand on the knob, ready to burst in—then stopped. *Wait a minute—what am I doing?* She looked at the door, imagining what was happening on the other side. *I'm an analyst! Not a damn shooter!* She started to back away when a thought struck her. *Waylon.* She saw Grigg's face in her mind's eye. *He was an analyst too—but he got killed in a situation a lot like this one.* She nodded slowly. *He was there to cover his partners—the agents he had led to that suspect.* She looked at the door. *I have a partner too*, she thought, and turned the knob. *And he's out there.*

She opened the door.

And found herself in the middle of a totally chaotic situation. Men, women, children—all were pushing and shoving their way toward the elevator, tearing at each other to get inside first.

Behind them, Flame, his face covered in blood, was looking down at the supine form of Samira. Dana could see that the girl was wearing a bomb vest that her partner was examining. *He should wait for the bomb squad,* she thought, then realized that there were no police—not even park officers— anywhere in sight. *I wonder if the admiral called them off.*

It didn't matter. What did matter was the people—they had to get the people safely out of here. Dana stepped forward, holding the door open and yelled: "Hey! Over here!"

People turned to look at her.

"Go down the stairs!" She nodded toward the open door. "Get out of here now!"

A chunk of the crowd started to move toward her.

"Go!" She gestured a middle-aged man in. "Get downstairs and out of the building." She waved her arm. "GO!"

People began to stream by her, heading for the staircase and safety. Dana let them go, turning toward Flame who was still examining the bomb vest.

She could see him touch something on the vest, something small and rectangular.

It's a cell phone, Dana realized. *A remote detonator.* She looked around. *The Statue is a huge Faraday cage; there's no way that anyone could detonate from outside.* She looked at the crowd still surging past her. *That means there's someone else in here.* She stepped to the side, began searching the faces all around her. *Who could it be?*

Her eyes roved from side to side, scanning the faces, checking for suspicious looks, odd movements. She was used to this kind of operation—after all, she was an analyst.

She took another long step to the side, separating herself from the hurrying crowd. She saw their frightened faces—and disregarded them. *The one I'm looking for won't be frightened,* she thought. *He'll be determined...*

She heard a commotion behind her then, turned just in time to see a man push his way through the crowd on the stairs—against the flow.

Who...?

He burst through the doorway, pushing people aside—one older man staggered to the side, crashed into Dana.

Both of them fell to the floor.

I know that man. Dana's eyes were locked on the man in the doorway. *It's the cabdriver.* She searched for his name. *Budayl Al Hakam Samaha.* She shook her head. *He's gotta be working with the girl.* She tried to push the old man away but he seemed stunned and his dead weight was pinning her to the floor. She saw Samaha pull out a cell phone and knew what he was going to do. *Can't let him use that!* She pushed at the old man—to no avail.

"FLAME!" She yelled the word as loud as she could—and realized it wasn't loud enough.

Samaha was pushing numbers on the phone. *He's going to blow the device!*

Dana looked around and saw the people still fleeing down the stairs, the people crowded around the elevator entrance. *They won't make it out in time.* Her eyes flickered to Flame. *Neither will he.*

There was only one thing to do. She reached into her purse, pulled out her pistol...

Flame says these things are accurate inside twenty feet or so. The cabdriver was only about ten feet away. *I hope he's right.* Dana braced herself as best she could, steadying the butt of the little Smith & Wesson in her hands.

She flicked the safety to off, took a deep breath and squeezed…

BLAM! The first shot surprised her—the retort, magnified and echoing through the large room was much louder than it had been when she'd been wearing ear protectors on the range. *Can't let that bother me.* She centered the sights on the cabdriver's turning head, squeezed again…

BLAM! This time she kept her focus on the target—and saw an explosion of red as her bullet caught him in the forehead. *I got him!* She watched him crumple to the floor. *I really got him!*

She finally managed to push herself free, took a long moment to stare at the gun in her hand, then carefully set the safety and walked up to the bloody body. She took the cell phone out of his hand and carefully cleared the number he'd been dialing before switching it off.

Chapter 25

There were FBI agents, Homeland Security Agents and a slope-shouldered representative from the State Department waiting for Dana and Flame when they came out of the Statue's pedestal. Flame had Samira walking in front of them, her hands tied with the scarf she had been wearing. Dana had the explosive belt, gingerly carrying it in over her slightly outstretched left arm. She didn't trust her hands, which were shaking uncontrollably.

Flame had been careful to disconnect both detonators before removing the belt from Samira but Dana would not feel really safe until it was in the hands of the bomb squad—and far away from her.

"Are you Dana Morton," the lead FBI agent stepped forward, signaling for an armored and padded member of the bomb squad to join him, "and Randall O'Donnell?"

"That's us," Flame glanced at the wall of agents in front of him. "What kept you guys?"

"I told them to hold back." The tall form of Admiral Dorrance stepped out from behind a group of agents. "I thought you'd do better if you didn't have to deal with Park Rangers getting in your way."

"You were right about that, sir." Flame stood just a little straighter as he addressed the admiral. SEAL etiquette required that he not come to attention—but he wasn't a SEAL anymore and he really did respect this man. "It *was* better with just the two of us." He nodded at Dana who was preoccupied as she gave the vest to the man from the bomb squad. "She did really well in there." He smiled. "Saved my ass for sure."

"I'm sure you both did exemplary work." He grinned. "You know, the State Department tried to stop me from coming here—said that we would embarrass the young lady and wreak havoc on the UN council meeting she was here for." His grin widened. "So I told them to send a rep with us—make sure we didn't 'embarrass' their precious guest." He gestured and the slope-shouldered man—the same State Department flunky who had accompanied them at the airport—was nudged forward by one of the FBI men. "What do you think, Dickson? Who did we embarrass?"

"I don't understand." He shook his head. "I…we thoroughly checked her out." The man kept his gaze on the ground as he spoke. "We had letters from her friends, her pastor…"

He stole a glance at the two. "There were no indications that Ms. Potros was anything but what she claimed to be—you have my word on that."

"Thanks a bunch, Bud." Flame shook his head. "That really makes me feel better." He gestured toward the knot of people on the dock, held there by the police and FBI. "I'm sure they feel the same way."

"Yes, well…" He coughed into his hand. "We would appreciate it if you would not tell the press about this." He finally looked up, his expression that of a man who has bitten into a lemon. "You will, of course, be paid the contract fee in full." He looked at the admiral who had raised an eyebrow. "With a bonus as a thank you."

"Okay." Flame turned his attention from the slope-shouldered man to the admiral. "What do *you* want us to do with her, sir?" Flame nodded toward Samira who was standing between two FBI men, her broken nose swollen to the point where she was almost unrecognizable.

"The FBI will take charge of her." Admiral Dorrance gestured. "It's a shame you couldn't keep her contact alive."

"Admiral, if he was still alive, a whole bunch of us would be dead and that Statue," he gestured over his shoulder at Lady Liberty, "might be lying right where we're standing. Flame put his hand on Dana's shoulder, inadvertently smearing some blood onto her blouse. "My partner," he smiled and rubbed the blood in. "Did a great job making sure that didn't happen."

"I'm glad." The admiral signaled to the FBI and one of the agents took charge of Samira. "Because I need you two to do something else for me." He led them away from the crowd. "That information you passed along about Mr. Mapache and Cobalt-60." He hesitated for a second. "We need to talk about that."

A short walk took them to the admiral's helicopter which lifted off as soon as they were aboard, headed for the midtown skyport. The three of them put on comm units, Dana requiring a little help from Flame—her hands were shaking too badly to allow her to properly position the earpieces.

When she was ready, the admiral made sure they were not on the general feed before he spoke.

"Now," he told them. "We've looked into the data that you got from the German reporter, and discovered that Ms. Hachtel was correct—the Cobalt-60 stolen in Northern Mexico was *not* recovered."

"But I saw the newspaper reports..." Dana leaned forward so she could see the admiral's face. "They put the robbers in a hospital, said they were exposed—contaminated."

"The Mexican authorities arrested the 'usual suspects' who, I suspect, were guilty only of being in the wrong place at the wrong time." He took a long breath. "My information is that they actually recovered less than a single gram of the Cobalt— the rest is missing." He shook his head. "To make matters worse, there was another robbery a few days later in which another sixty grams were stolen and a driver murdered." He looked into both their faces. "*That*was never reported."

"So Karin...excuse me, Ms. Hachtel's fears are well founded?"

"Her uncle was most certainly assassinated. His car was blown to pieces with what appears to be a military-grade explosive of some kind." The admiral looked grim. "And his replacement recently ordered seventy-five grams of Cobalt-60 from a hospital supplier in San Antonio."

"You're going to stop the order, right?"

"We can't do that." The admiral's face went grimmer still. "Our 'friends' in the State Department are unwilling to believe that our Mexican 'allies' would lie to us. They're afraid any action we take will hurt relations." He snorted.

"So what are you going to do?" Flame thought he had an idea of what his former boss might have in mind.

"I'm going to ask you two to go in and investigate. Take the German girl with you—she'll be your cover. As far as everyone is concerned, it's her investigation and you two are just going along as security."

"I don't know if she'll go for that..."

"It was her uncle that died." The admiral turned to Dana. "Appeal to her family pride."

"I think it's better that Flame handle that," Dana nodded to her partner. "He already has a rapport with Ms. Hachtel..."

"So be it." The admiral leaned back in his seat. "I can't give you any official support." He held up a hand into which his aide put a small device. "I can give you this satellite phone. It'll connect directly to my office." He handed it to Flame. "Use it and I'll send what help I can."

"Intel?" That from Dana.

"I'll see to it that a satellite is parked above the area you're working in. My aide will give you operational details and passwords." He looked at the two of them. "Anything else?"

"Well, sir." Dana dipped her eyes, "I have to ask..." She looked up. "Who's paying for all this?"

"Your fees will be picked up by my office." He smiled. "Don't go overboard on expenses, please."

"No sir," Dana shook her head. "We won't, sir."

"Good," the admiral peered out the window. "We're about to set down—I will not be debarking here." He held out a hand. "Be careful, both of you." He smiled. "And for God's sake, get that blood off before too many people see it!"

***

"Okay," Flame was still towel-drying his wet hair as he stepped into the shared living room of their suite. "Karin is still in the hotel and she's agreed to meet me for dinner later tonight."

"That's good," Dana had just had her own shower. She held up her bloodstained blouse. "Flame," she looked into his face, "you did this on purpose, didn't you?"

"Well..."

"Come on, don't bullshit me—we're partners, right?"

"Okay," he grinned sheepishly. "I did smear you on purpose." He hung the towel over his shoulders. "When I was young, my Dad and some of his buddies would go hunting." He shrugged. "They'd go after all kinds of things—deer, raccoon, rabbit—whatever was plentiful and edible." He smiled. "I'll tell you, some of them had odd ideas on what was edible and what wasn't!"

He looked at Dana. "Anyway, when someone new went along—somebody's son or a flier that had just moved in—they'd take him along and, if he managed to shoot whatever it was they were hunting for, they'd hold a little ceremony." He smiled, remembering. "They'd smear some blood from the kill on his face—tell him he'd been 'blooded'—and give him the meat for his own kitchen."

"And that's why…"

"You'd been properly blooded," he shrugged. "And I didn't think you'd like it if I smeared blood on your face." He gave her another sheepish grin. "I thought the blouse would be okay—I'll buy you a new one if you want."

"No," Dana shook her head slowly. "That's all right." She noticed a spot of blood on his hand. "It looks like that butterfly bandage slipped while you were in the shower." She moved closer, sitting on the coffee table and holding out her hands. "Let's see it."

"It's nothing." He showed her his left hand. "Really, not deep enough to be a threat."

"Okay," she nodded. "I'll look at it in the morning and see if we need to do anything to it."

"That'll work." Flame started to get up, thought of something and looked down at his partner. "Listen." He gently touched her shoulder. "I know I'm not the proper person to say this," he smiled. "But if you need to talk about what happened…"

"Not yet, Flame." Dana made an almost invisible negating motion with her hand. "I'll let you know if I have any problems."

"Do that." He turned toward his own room. "I'm going to get dressed and see if I can talk our German friend into being our 'beard.'"

"I don't think you'll have any trouble," Dana stood and headed to the desk where her laptop sat. "Meanwhile, I'll check out all the data the admiral's aide passed along and make sure all the codes are good."

"See you later," Flame paused at the doorway. "And don't forget what I said."

"I won't." Dana powered up the computer. "I promise I won't."

***

Dana settled in working at her computer. The codes the admiral had given her opened up vistas of raw data that she'd been denied access to for weeks. She tried to lose herself in the flow of information—but her mind kept circling back to the events of the day that had just ended.

She looked down at the bloodstained blouse on her lap. *I killed a man today.* Her mind replayed the scene—the panicked civilians running for the staircase. Flame fighting to deactivate the explosive vest as the cabdriver prepared to remotely detonate it.

She remembered the feel of the pistol in her hand. Saw the dot of her front sight touch the man's head…

Once again she heard the thunder of the shot, felt the recoil as the weapon jumped in her hands…

Saw the cabdriver's head explode as her carefully aimed round found its target.

Flame is right. She pushed back from the computer. *It's going to be difficult for me to process this.* She took in a long breath. *I'm a different person now.* She ran her fingers over the dark stain. *I'm blooded.* She let that thought sink in. *I killed a man—and I'm going to have to learn to live with it.*

She sat back. *Can I do that?* She looked out onto the city and let her mind race. *Can I?*

***

Downstairs, Flame was doing his best to charm the German reporter as the two of them shared an overpriced hotel meal.

"We passed the information about your uncle Axel to some people working in the intelligence community…"

"And you found?"

"The explosion that killed your uncle was no accident." Flame kept his tone as unemotional as he could. "The police there are trying to cover up what was clearly an assassination."

"I see," Karin's eyes filled. "They killed him because he wouldn't co-operate." She reached out for Flame's hand. "What can I do? How can I get justice for my uncle?"

"Not from the Mexican authorities." Flame held her hand, leaned close. "That much is certain."

"How then?" Her lower lip trembled with emotion. "Will the US government help?"

"No." Flame shook his head. "Our current administration is more interested in maintaining relations than justice."

Karin nodded slowly in understanding, and then lifted her eyes. "Will you help, Flame?"

He smiled and nodded slowly. "Dana and I will both help if you're willing to take some risks to help *us*."

"Tell me!"

Flame carefully laid out the plan the admiral had outlined for him, telling the German reporter that she would appear to be entering Mexico to start her own investigation— with Flame and Dana along to cover her and nudge the investigation in the proper direction if they saw something she did not.

"I can't promise that there won't be any danger." Flame didn't want her to go into this blind. "But I *can* promise that I will do my best to keep you safe."

"Like you did in Iraq."

"Something like that."

"Thank you, Flame." She smiled and squeezed his hand. "Of course I will go to Mexico with you." Her smile widened. "And perhaps you will return the favor and come to my room tonight?"

She stood and drew him up with her. "I have waited too long to reward you for your courage in the desert."

***

It was near dawn when Flame returned to his room. Dana heard him enter—she hadn't managed much sleep. *How do Flame and the other SEALs do it?* She wondered. *How do they spill blood and still sleep peacefully?*

Of course, she knew that *Flame* didn't sleep too peacefully. *But that's only since the head wound he received in Mexico,* she told herself. *Before that...*

Before that, she suddenly realized, she had no idea how the man had slept.

I'll have to ask him, she decided. *Get him to tell me the secret of pushing the images down inside—penning them up so they won't come to me in my dreams.*

She hoped there *was* a way to do that—a secret that men like Flame learned in training or were told by other combat veterans.

Because if there isn't, if I have to learn to live with it by myself...

She didn't know what she would do if that was the case.

***

Flame slipped into his room as quietly as he could. Karin had been a demanding bed partner and Flame was still feeling the various wounds he had received at the Statue of Liberty— which he could not, of course, talk about.

There hadn't been much time for talk in any event. Karin had led him to her room and, turning to face him, had stripped herself naked. She had clearly been planning to do so—how else could one account for the total lack of any underwear?

"Come to me, my Flame." She backed away from him, heading for the king-sized bed that was the room's dominant feature. "Let me show you my appreciation for all that you have done for me." She licked her rather nicely shaped lips. "And what you have agreed to do with me," she smiled. "And for me in the days ahead."

Flame didn't need a whole lot of encouragement—it had been a while since his adventures on Virginia Beach. He took a moment to hang out the 'DO NOT DISTURB' sign, then followed the brunette to the big bed where he soon found that he hadn't lost his touch...

***

He left some hours later. Karin was sleeping the sleep of exhaustion and would probably do so until her wake-up call came in. Flame thought, for a moment, of going out for a run.

No, he finally decided. *I should try to get some sleep. Tomorrow is going to be a long day of preparation and the day after,* he stifled a yawn, *is going to be longer still.*

He bypassed the elevator, jogged up the stairs to his floor. *Manny used to tell us all to rest when we had the opportunity.* He came to the door that led to his floor, stared at it for a long moment, then pushed it open. *I think he might have been right.* He yawned as he unlocked the door to his bedroom and tossed his clothes onto the chair next to the bed, ignoring the shirt that missed and fell to the floor.

Now, let's see if I can *sleep!* He put his own 'DO NOT DISTURB' sign out, pushed the air conditioner's setting to 'Stun' and crawled under the covers.*No dreams tonight.* He closed his eyes. *Please!*

Chapter 26

A few thousand miles and several time zones away, a NAFTA-licensed truck sat, motor running, in the loading dock of Metropolitan Methodist Hospital in San Antonio, Texas. The driver had been charged with transporting seventy-five grams of Cobalt-60 to the oncological unit at Doctor's Hospital in Monterrey, Mexico—a seven or eight hour trip.

He'd taken his time preparing for the trip, making sure that all the paperwork was in order—the drive itself was long enough without spending hours at the Nuevo Laredo border crossing trying to explain why he was taking radioactive material across the border.

Not part of my job description, he told himself. *Just make sure the paperwork is all here and the rest of the trip is all downhill.* He smiled. *Except for the parts where I have to go uphill!*

He knew that he could take Route 85 for most of the trip, but the road wasn't always in the best repair—especially the parts beyond the border crossing.

Doesn't matter. He took the last batch of papers from the dispatcher. *They're paying me almost double my usual rate for this run—seems the Mexican Hospital really needs the Cobalt stuff.* He headed for his truck. *I'll get it there for them.* He smiled. *And then blow off a little steam at one of them cantinas...*

He put the truck in gear and rolled out of the hospital parking lot, turning left and heading for the Route 85 on-ramp. He had a bunch of miles to cover and he wanted to finish before sundown.

***

"So." Flame piled lox, cream cheese and a slice of bacon onto his bagel, pushing down hard to keep the whole thing from exploding apart. "Karin has to cover the UN conference today. She's good to head down to Mexico anytime tomorrow." He took a bite of the concoction. "I assume you can find us transport?"

Dana frowned as he licked around the edges of the bagel, making sure he got all the oozing cheese. "How can you eat that?" She looked at her own bagel, modestly buttered. "I mean..."

"Hey," Flame held up a hand. "I did my weight training this morning—burned a whole lot of calories." He started to hold up the bagel, winced when the bacon slipped out. "I have to take in some food."

"If you say so," Dana shook her head. "As for the transport," she touched her laptop. "How would you like to go?"

"Commercial is best." Flame popped the bacon into his mouth. "Get us into Monterrey as directly as you can."

"I'm not sure how many flights go there…"

"Do your best," he took another bite of the bagel. "If there's nothing to Monterrey get us to San Antonio—we can drive from there."

"I'm worried about crossing the border…"

"You got all the licenses from State, right?"

"Of course," she looked at him. "But won't the Mexican border police be worried about whatever weapons we bring in?"

"Mexican border police can be bribed." He pulled another bagel from the bag and cut it in half. "So can customs agents." He reached for the cream cheese. "We won't have any trouble on that account."

Dana nodded, thought for a moment, then: "Flame?"

The redhead took a big bite of the second bagel then looked toward her and raised an eyebrow: "Uh?"

"I've…" Dana hesitated, wondering if this would drive a wedge between them. *Maybe he won't trust me to watch his back*, she thought to herself. *Maybe…*

She pushed the maybes aside with an effort and looked into Flame's forthright green eyes.

"Flame," she took a deep breath. "How do you live with it?"

He swallowed his bagel. "Killin' that guy is bothering you, right?"

She nodded.

"Dana, you've gotta be careful how you look at things." He sipped his coffee. "Those three wanted to kill a lot of people, a lot of kids out on a holiday—and why did they want to do that? Because they're crazies who want to destroy everything that civilization has built in the last four hundred years." He shook his head and leaned forward. "I've seen things that you wouldn't believe. In Iraq, I saw babies and young kids sliced to pieces because their parents believed that the Prophet wanted his wife's father to be his successor instead of some other guy. I saw a young woman stoned to death because she took a chocolate bar from an American soldier. ..." He turned his eyes to the wall as memories welled up. "I've seen whole villages slaughtered because they gave water to some passing American troops." He shook his head. "The people who did things like that don't deserve our consideration. They don't deserve our concern." He looked into Dana's eyes. "Hell, they don't deserve to be thought of as people—that's why my brothers and I give them other names—skinny, hadji, raghead..."

"They hurt innocents and it's our job to stop them." He took her hands in his. "They're targets, Dana, just targets. Don't think of them any other way."

He smiled. "Do you understand that?"

"I think so."

"Just remember why we do this—why we got put in the position where we have to do it." He took her hand. "Remember those planes with all those innocent people on board that they used on 9/11. That guy in the Statue was trying to do the same sort of thing—kill a bunch of people to prove that his God is best. He *chose* to do that and by doing so, put himself in the line of fire." He squeezed her trembling hand. "You did the right thing. You must *know* that. You did the only thing any sane person could do."

"Thanks," Dana pulled her hand away, turned to look out the window. "I think that helps..."

"Good." He smiled and took another bagel. "Now finish your breakfast and let's go to work!"

***

When she returned to work, Dana found to her surprise that Monterrey was home to the General Mariano Escobedo International Airport, which was considered one of the most modern airports in North America. They would have to change at Houston but there were plenty of flights to that city.

She booked seats for the three of them to fly out on Friday morning.

Flame made a list of the equipment and supplies he thought they'd need once they reached Mexico. Some of it he had on hand, the rest he was able to get from his friend Bremby. It would all be shipped via Federal Express—the best way to get weapons through customs.

All would be waiting at their hotel—the Four Points Sheraton—which was convenient to both the hospital and the town's center.

Satisfied that everything at his end was in order, Flame changed and headed out for a run. Dana considered joining him but decided, instead, to return to the computer and see what she could find out from various intelligence sources. It was detail-oriented work and she hoped it would tire her out enough to allow her to sleep.

She worked at it for nearly three hours, especially looking for informational details on Mapache and his gang—the DEA had quite a complete file on him and Dana pulled in all the data she could including the places he and his people could usually be found. *We're going to need that.* As she copied the data, a minor computer notation caught her eye. *Mapache was arrested a week or so ago,* she noted. *And he made a phone call while he was in the local jail.* She pulled up NSA's intel site. *I wonder what he wanted to talk about...*

***

Flame had just finished his run and returned to his room when Dana knocked on the door.

"What's up?" he asked, stripping off his sweat-soaked shirt. "I was just gonna shower."

"I found something." She gestured toward her computer. "Something you should see." She led him back to the table, called up the file she had found and hit play.

"Matias?" The voice was Mapache's, garbled but legible. "The doctor is being unreasonable." There was a long pause, then: "You will handle it? Good, perhaps his replacement can be made to see reason."

The connection clicked as it closed.

"So he did have Karin's uncle killed," Flame sat back on the couch. "Bastard."

"There's more than that," Dana sat across from him. "The other man—Matias—I did a search with some new voice recognition software and came up with something." She pulled up another file on the computer and placed it on the coffee table in front of him. "For the past few years, Iran has made efforts to infiltrate several Latin American countries—they've installed secret intelligence and training centers where they take in converts to Islam and teach them how to commit acts of international terrorism."

"Manny told us something about that when we first started briefing in on the Mexican Operation..."

"One of their organizations blew up a Jewish Center in Buenos Aires," she frowned. "Eighty-five people were killed. Just three years ago, they tried to use a drug cartel to assassinate a Saudi diplomat."

"Yeah," Flame nodded. "I heard about that one while I was in Afghanistan."

"The president signed the 'Countering Iran in the Western Hemisphere Act' into law last year to try to assess Iranian-related threats in Central and South America."

"And what does all of this have to do with us?"

"Matias Blanco—the other voice on that phone call—is one of the leaders of the biggest terrorist group in Argentina. He converted to Islam nearly fifteen years ago but hasn't taken a Muslim name." She shook her head. "Thinks it might compromise his effectiveness."

"Pretty smart."

"If Mapache is working with him, it's likely that they have something big in mind." Dana searched Flame's face. "Can we handle it alone?"

"We're gonna have to." Flame shrugged. "You heard what the admiral said."

"Okay," Dana matched his shrug with one of her own. "Now, the next question—are you going to tell Ms. Hachtel what I found?"

"Would it violate NSA security in any way?"

"Not after all of Edward Snowden's leaks."

"Then I think I will tell her." He nodded to himself. "She deserves to know who we're dealing with."

"All right." Dana picked up the laptop and headed back to the desk. "I'll see what else I can find out."

"I'll grab a shower while you're doing that—then we go to lunch." He smiled and headed into his room. "I have something really special in mind."

***

"Pizza?" Dana asked an hour later. "You take me out to lunch and we have pizza?"

"Not just any pizza," Flame grinned. "This is Famous Ray's—the best pizza in the world!" He gestured around him. "Look at how crowded it is! New Yorker's really know their pizza."

"I prefer Chicago deep dish myself."

"Are you crazy?" Flame shook his head. "You just get a whole mess of extra tomato sauce and it's impossible to eat with your hand. Look," he picked up a piece, folded it, and bit off the end—and looked surprised. "Hey!" He grinned. "It tastes like pizza!"

"Glad to hear it." Dana actually quite liked pizza—she was just giving her partner a hard time for the hell of it. *He just wanted to get me out of the hotel for a while,* she told herself. *Give me a chance to relax.* She smiled. *And he's done just that!*

She picked up another piece of pizza, folded it the way he had showed her, and took a big bite.

It tasted just fine.

When they were done, Flame took her on a walk. Ray's was right on the edge of Greenwich Village and there were lots of things to see and do in the area. He led them through Washington Square Park, where students from nearby NYU threw Frisbees, smoked pot and argued about the state of the world.

The Strand, the largest bookstore in the United States was his last stop. It carried every kind of book published and Dana spent more than an hour poking through the shelves. She knew she'd have to come back here one day and buy some books for the small but select library she kept in her D.C. apartment.

From the Strand, Flame took her, tired but happy, back into the subway and uptown.

"Thank you, Flame," Dana said to him as they sat down in the subway car.

"For what?"

"For forcing me to take a break and giving me a chance to let off some steam." She looked at him and smiled. "I really needed it." Her smile widened. "Now I understand some of the things you guys have done after a mission."

"It's important to let yourself stand down." Flame nodded slowly, "You can't stay 'up' all the time."

"How do *you* let off steam?"

He raised an eyebrow and looked down at her. "I think you know perfectly well how I let off steam!"

"Last night help?"

"Yep," he smiled. "And I'm kinda hoping tonight will be just as good."

"I'll remember to leave when the time comes."

"You do that." His smile widened. "It's what partners are supposed to do!"

They smiled and chatted through the rest of the ride, getting back to the hotel relaxed and refreshed with time for a nap before meeting Karin for dinner.

Flame was pretty certain neither of them would have to worry about bad dreams this afternoon...

Chapter 27

They had to hurry to catch their flight to Houston. A traffic jam in the midtown tunnel delayed their shuttle badly enough to force them to run to reach their gate.

Dana had been concerned that they'd be stopped at the security gate—after all, they had checked two weapons at the curb—but apparently the paperwork from the State Department was enough to get them through and they reached their gate just in time to board their flight.

"So what do we do when we get to Monterrey?" Karin asked when the plane was airborne. "You said that you wanted me to get aggressive." She grinned showing white and even teeth. "Or was that just for last night!"

Dana smiled. She had seen the claw marks on Flame's shoulder as they finished packing their gear that morning—and had known where they came from.

"We want you to interrogate the new hospital administrator, one Dr. Antonio Calvera for openers," Dana had pulled his name from the internet. "Calvera doesn't really have the credentials or the experience to run a hospital—and his name was pushed through by the ruling board in quite a hurry." She smiled. "Wouldn't that seem suspicious to an investigative reporter looking into her uncle's death?"

"It would indeed." Karin had opened her laptop and was taking notes. "What do I want this Calvera to tell me?"

"I doubt he'll tell you anything of importance." Dana shrugged. "I doubt that he knows anything."

"If he does," Karin nodded, "he *will* tell me—I guarantee it."

"Whatever." Dana waved that aside. "What we hope he does is yell for help from this Mapache character."

"Who will then try to blow me up as he did Uncle Axel."

"He might try," Flame put in. "But we won't let that happen."

"What we *will* do is grab whoever he sends and use him to reach Mapache."

"And from Mapache to Blanco." Karin nodded. "It is classic."

"We have to do it quickly." Dana frowned as she looked at her laptop. "It seems that another truckload of Cobalt-60 crossed the border yesterday." She looked at Flame. "Destination: the Doctor's Hospital of Monterrey."

The three of them looked at one another—and began to think about the mission ahead...

***

General Mariano Escobedo International Airport was just as modern and efficient as advertised. A twenty-minute cab ride delivered them to the front door of their hotel where all three took quick showers and changed into fresh clothes. By agreement, Karin and Dana headed for the nearby Doctor's Hospital while Flame tracked down the parcels sent from Garland Bremby's shop.

Doctor's Hospital was a large, modern looking group of buildings attached to a very large parking garage. The two girls headed for the main entrance and, once inside, to the oversized reception desk.

"We would like to see Dr. Antonio Calvera," Karin told the petite brunette behind the desk.

"Do you have an appointment?" She looked the two women up and down, measuring them. One was clearly an Anglo, but the other?

"Tell him it is a matter of some urgency." Karin passed the girl her card. "Tell him I am the niece of his predecessor."

"You are related to Dr. Farber?" The girl's expression changed, brightened. "He was such a wonderful man. The way he died…"

"It is about that I wish to speak to Dr. Calvera." Karin leaned forward. "Can you tell him I am here?"

"Of course, *senorita*! I will be glad to." She reached for a house phone. "If you would, please take a seat over there," she pointed to the large waiting room just off the main entrance. "I promise you it will not be for long."

Karin and Dana did as she asked, sitting, coincidentally, in the very seats Mapache and his men had occupied just a week or so earlier.

They had barely settled themselves when an elevator bell rang and the worried-looking figure of Dr. Calvera headed in their direction.

"*Senorita* Hachtel?" He stopped in front of Karin. "I am told you have questions about the fate of Dr. Farber?"

"I have many questions." Karin's eyes cut into the man. "Should I ask them here?" She looked around at the other people seated in the room. "Or do you have an office we might use."

"Of course," the doctor stepped back. "Excuse me!" He extended a welcoming hand. "Please, come this way." He led them back to the elevator. "Certainly we should be more comfortable while we talk."

The elevator door silently closed behind them.

As the girls made their way to Dr. Calvera's, Flame was entering his third office. The hotel's front desk had no record of any FedEx delivery for Randall O'Donnell—even though the FedEx internet site showed a delivery at 9 a.m. that very morning and a signature that seemed a match to the delivery room manager—something the young desk clerk could not explain.

Flame had, rather politely, requested a manager—and gotten the same answer. A second manager passed him to the hotel's general manager who lobbed him back to the delivery room.

Flame was ready to wring the truth out of the next person who told him they didn't have his delivery.

That didn't happen. The three large boxes Bremby had sent out were in a security cage just off the loading dock. The clerk working there couldn't explain how the front desk didn't know of their existence—she had sent the paperwork their way as soon as the parcels arrived.

Flame nodded and asked that all three parcels be delivered to his room—with him accompanying them to make sure they didn't go missing again.

The clerk called for a burly worker who packed the parcels—rather roughly—onto a wheeled cart and led Flame through the bowels of the hotel to the employee-only elevator that whisked them up to a corridor that connected with the hallway right across from Flame's room.

From there it took only a moment to unload. Flame passed the man a US twenty, smiled at him—and closed the door in his face.

He didn't expect to need any of the gear here—but he'd want it ready in any event—it never hurt to be prepared.

***

"…You are trying to tell me that you have no idea what happened to my uncle," Karin was leaning forward in her chair, eyes burning holes in Dr. Calvera's trembling form. "His car just exploded—on its own." She shook her head. "Do cars explode here all the time? How often does it happen?" She turned to Dana. "Make a note on that, it might make an interesting presentation—'The City of Exploding Cars.'"

It had been decided that Dana would play Karin's assistant—it would allow the analyst a measure of anonymity to study the faces and movements of people while *their* attention was centered on Karin.

"Did the police declare it 'just' an exploding car?" Karin pressed her advantage. "What kinds of cars are most susceptible to explosion? Are Mercedes safer than Fords?"

"Please, *Senorita*, I know nothing about this."

"My uncle devoted his life to this hospital. He was instrumental in raising the funding to build it—now you sit in his office and tell me you don't have any idea how he died other then: 'his car exploded'?" She snorted. "Are you really going to tell me that?"

"*Senorita*," Calvera looked around his office, searching for what, he didn't really know. "*Senorita*, your uncle was a very fine man—a man I admired very much. What happened to him…" He shook his head. "I cannot tell you how much I regret what happened." He wrung his hands together. "But I can tell you nothing. There are bad men involved—men who would hurt you if they thought I told you anything about them."

I'll be damned, Dana thought. *She got him to open up!* Dana would have been willing to bet almost anything that the man would never say a word—he was too obviously terrified. *Karin should get a new job.* Dana hid a smile. *The CIA could use someone like her.*

Calvera was almost babbling now, begging Karin to leave things alone before something happened to her. The German let him spout, then cut him off with one cuttingly-delivered word.

"Enough!" She stared at him as he stopped in mid-sentence, mouth half open. "It's clear that you know a lot more than you have said about my uncle's death." She leaned forward and put her hands on his desk. "It is also clear that you are afraid to tell me anything that might lead me to the truth."

"Please, *senorita*…" Calvera shrunk back into his over-padded chair.

"No," Karin made a cutting gesture in the air between them. "I will listen to no more from you—someone who betrayed a man he says he respected and admired." She stood. "I will have to go to the Federal Police now, perhaps when I tell them what you have told me…"

"No *senorita*," Calvera rushed to get in front of her, hand folded in a begging position. "The police have been bribed by this man! They will not go after him, instead, they will betray you and you will be killed! Please…"

"I don't believe it," Karin brushed past him. "This is a civilized country. I cannot believe that all the police are corrupt."

"*Senorita!*"

Karin slammed the door in his face.

"What do you think," she whispered to Dana as they headed to the elevator.

"I'm impressed." She smiled. "And I'd be willing to bet that he's calling someone in the police station right now!" Her smile widened. "We'll be able to tell for sure when we get back to the hotel." Dana made a gesture. "I planted a bug in his office."

"You Americans," Karin laughed. "It's just as Ms. Merkel says, you listen to everyone."

They stepped into the elevator, pressed the button for the ground floor. "Someday," Karin continued, "I will have to tell you what our secret service did to Number Ten Downing Street."

"I look forward to that." The elevator opened on the ground floor. "For now, we check my little bug, read Flame in on the current situation," Dana shrugged. "Then go talk to the police." She smiled. "With him covering us, of course."

"Of course."

The two waved to the girl at the reception desk and exited the building, side by side.

***

"They are coming to see you next, Captain," Dr. Calvera's voice was crystal clear as it issued from the speakers of Dana's laptop. "They want more information about what happened to Dr. Farber. I couldn't stop them!"

"Fool!" The new voice was in a lower register and exhibited more control. "You know that most of my men do not know what's going on—you also know what Mapache said would happen to the two of us if anyone interfered now!"

"You can stop them from discovering anything." Calvera's voice was agitated, frightened. "You must stop them!"

"How would you suggest I do that?" The deep voice was level, unworried. "Should I kill them both? Perhaps arrange a car accident like the one that claimed the reporter's uncle?"

"They made fun of that," Calvera's voice was nearly hysterical now. "They said they'd do a television report on it— on a city where cars just 'blow up.'"

"They won't get the chance." The voice was flat and certain. "I'll take care of them—don't worry about it."

"But the shipment…"

"The shipment is safe for now—make sure it stays that way."

"I will, I promise…"

"I will hold you to that promise," the voice was sharp now. "And join you tomorrow to make sure the shipment goes out as planned."

"Tomorrow."

There was a click and Dana cut the computer playback. "That's it," she looked at her two companions. "Whoever that was in the police station will 'take care' of us."

"And the Cobalt is due to be turned over to this Mapache tomorrow." Flame nodded. "We're going to have to hurry if we're going to intercept it."

"What do you think we should do?" Karin sounded worried. "Should we call for help?"

"Not yet." Flame turned to Dana. "Got a plan, partner?"

"I do," she looked into Flame's face. "But it's going to be up to you to make sure it doesn't blow up in our faces."

"Let's hear it."

Dana nodded and leaned closer to her two companions, detailing what she had in mind…

***

Dana and Karin waited until after siesta time, when the sun began to go down, before they headed for the police station. The extra time allowed Flame to make his preparations while forcing the captain to sweat it out a little while longer.

The police station was a modern building—two stories tall with a single-story garage in the back. Various lights went on as the sun dipped below the horizon.

"If this is like stations in the US, there'll be a sergeant on duty at a desk in the front." Dana held the door for Karin. "We see him first." She smiled. "Go easy on him."

"Got it."

The interior set-up was pretty much what Dana expected. A sergeant sat at a slightly raised desk, two closed doors behind him.

He looked up as they approached.

"¿Cómo puedo ayudar a ustedes, señoras?"

"Good evening," Karin smiled at the slightly overweight policeman. "We would like to speak to your captain. Is he here?"

"¿Qué es esto?" He hesitated. "Excuse me—my English is not good." He shrugged. "What is…what is it about?"

"My name is Karin Hachtel. My uncle was Dr. Axel Farber—administrator of the Doctor's Hospital." She nodded in the appropriate direction. "He was killed recently and I have questions about what happened."

"*Si,*" the sergeant nodded. "I knew Dr. Farber—he was a good man. He fixed my son's broken leg." He shook his head. "His death—it was a terrible thing."

"It was." Karin nodded in turn. "Can we see the captain to talk about it?"

"Of course!" The man picked up a phone on his desk, muttered a few words into it, then smiled and stepped down from his desk and opened one of the two doors behind it. "He is in his office—he says he has been waiting for you." The man pointed. "Just go to the end of this hall."

"Thank you, sergeant." Karin smiled and touched his hand. "You have been most helpful."

She held the smile while he closed the door. "Okay," she nodded. "He's back at his desk."

"Flame?" Dana activated the ear bug she had inserted before going into the station. "The captain's office is at the left—back of the building."

There was a blip as Flame tapped on his own earbud.

"Okay, he's on the move." Dana gestured down the hall. "It's time for us to see the captain."

***

It took Flame a few minutes to find the main power line for the police station. *I wonder who writes their building code,* he asked himself when he discovered the line he was looking for was actually shared by several buildings, the transformer and circuit boxes for all of them in a single location—underground—right next to the gas line. *I mean, one short circuit and...*

He remembered a case some years back where a Mexican City had built a subway line and, in the process, screwed up a feeder and filled their sewers with gasoline. *Whole town blew up.* He shook his head. National Geographic *did a whole TV thing about it.*

The electrical system he was looking at could do much the same thing. *I was gonna blow the box for the police station and go from there,* Flame thought. *Now I guess I'm just gonna have to settle for a single cable.* He traced the lines from the transformer. *This one here.*

He pulled a bit of C-4 off the brick he had in his backpack, rolled it into wormlike shape, than carefully wrapped it around the line he'd chosen—as far from the gas line as he could manage.

Now to insert the detonator... He set the frequency carefully—*don't want a stray signal to set it off*—and closed the access panel. *Now I just have to wait for Dana's signal.*

It came seconds later: "The captain's office is at the left—back of the building."

Flame tapped his earbud to inform Dana he'd gotten her signal and headed for the rear of the police station.

***

"Ladies," said Captain Enrique Jesus Monasterio, the fifth of his line to hold the rank but the first to actually make any money out of it.

"What can I do to help you?" He smiled and gestured to the chairs placed in front of his desk.

"My uncle," Karin leaned forward. "Dr. Farber…"

"A wonderful man!" Monasterio nodded in admiration. "Such a shame that he died in such a way."

"Yes, in an 'accidental' explosion." Karin glared at him. "I understand such things are common around here."

"Of course not," Monasterio waved the concept away. "He was assassinated by a criminal gang—perhaps one of the Cartels." He nodded. "I am not such a fool that I cannot see that." He leaned forward conspiratorially. "But we cannot let the people of Monterrey know that such things happen in their own community—there would be unrest…"

"So you are investigating his death?"

"Of course!" The captain smiled a glaringly white smile. "Even as we speak…"

Before Karin could say another word, the room shook to a thunderous explosion.

***

Flame was thrown off balance as something large blew up. He'd been about to set off his own explosion—one that would have cut the power to the police station. He would then have seized the captain so they could squeeze the information they needed out of him.

Not gonna work now, Flame decided and turned toward the growing fire caused by the explosion. *Looks like the hospital,* a thought struck him. *I wonder if another administrator just "accidentally" died in an exploding car.*

He headed back to the hotel—it wouldn't do to be caught in the street with a brick of C-4 now.

***

Dana saw the very real surprise in the captain's face at the sound of the explosion. *He didn't know that was coming,* she realized. *It was a shock to him.*

She turned to Karin, afraid that the German reporter would think that the blast was part of their plan—but the other girl had immediately realized what had really happened.

"Another exploding car?" Karin raised an eyebrow. "Perhaps my network should do a documentary about this place."

"You will excuse me, ladies." Monasterio headed for the door, grabbing his hat as he went. "I must investigate this!"

The two watched as he exited, then Dana slipped a tiny bit of metal from her bag, removed a paper backing, and stuck it to the base of the captain's phone.

"Never waste an opportunity," she told Karin as the two of them headed back down the hall. "You never know what you might find out."

***

"I think Mapache beat us to the punch." Flame was already in their hotel suite, tossing gear into a backpack. "Check your bug."

Dana opened her laptop, punched in a code. "There was a call." She pulled up the file. "Incoming." She opened the file: "I have a truck on the way." The voice was low-pitched and very, very sure of itself. "Make sure the shipment is ready for pick-up." There was a long pause before Calvera's voice, shaky with nerves, answered: "It will be ready."

"Good," the low-pitched voice seemed pleased. "Once you are sure of that, go to your car and drive home." There was a hint of a laugh. "You have to have an alibi—stay above suspicion." This time there was a laugh. "Far above suspicion!"

The call cut out.

"The Cobalt-60's gone by now," Flame shook his head. "And we don't have a clue in which direction."

"We'll get one." Dana looked thoughtful. "If they took out the doctor, they're eliminating loose ends."

"And?"

"There's one left."

"Captain Monasterio," Karin nodded. "Of course! The explosion surprised him—I could see that in his face."

"Does he have a car?" Flame put in.

Dana stood. "Let's go and ask him."

"Not us," Karin stood. "Me—I think I know just how to handle it…"

***

Captain Monasterio was staring at a hole in the hospital parking lot. Flaming debris was all around, some of which had broken one of the hospital windows and started another fire inside.

The local fire department was doing its best to deal with both blazes although the bulk of their attention was directed at the interior blaze, which was threatening to spread.

"Another exploding car, eh Captain?" In all the chaos and confusion, Monasterio had failed to see Karin as she approached him. "Perhaps this is a special kind of city," she smiled at him. "Or perhaps someone is just tying up loose ends."

"What do you mean?" That last remark had come a bit too close to home for the captain.

"You know what I mean," the German shook her head slowly. "The killing of a beloved doctor, the theft of a quantity of Cobalt-60, all with the aid of another doctor and…" She stared at Monasterio. "The Captain of the city's police force."

"Are you accusing me of something, Senorita? Because if you are…"

"Captain, I do not care who you take money from—I really don't, but…" Karin's voice turned hard as steel. "If you had anything to do with the murder of my uncle, I will see you dead and in the ground."

"*Senorita…*"

"Do not deny knowing what I'm talking about, Captain. We're aware of your relationship with the late Doctor Calvera…" She nodded at the burning crater that had been the administrator's car. "We just want to know who you were working for," Her eyes burned into his. "And where the Cobalt-60 is headed."

"It's gone?"

"What do you think?"

Monasterio looked into the fire and thought about his next move. He could kill this annoying reporter. *But what would I gain from that?* He knew that she had a colleague with her and, for all he knew, that other woman might be watching this exchange even now. *It would just bring down more trouble— trouble I might not be able to handle.* He could contact Mapache, press the criminal for a bigger payoff now that the doctor was dead. *But I have no leverage—especially if the Cobalt really is gone.*

What did that leave him? What could he do?

Then the reporter gave him something else to worry about.

"What sort of car do you have, Captain?" She smiled sweetly. "I wonder if it too might suddenly explode." Her eyes caught his. "With you inside."

He wouldn't! Monasterio stared at what was left of Doctor Calvera and considered his position as the last remaining loose end…

* * *

"They're heading west," Karin told Dana upon her return to the room. "Mapache is taking the Cobalt to a farm just south of Ensenada—the rest of it is already there." She looked around. "Where is Flame?"

"He'll meet us at the car." Dana packed a last few items into her bag. "I arranged a rental—it's downstairs." Karin retrieved her own bag and, a few minutes later, the two girls were out of the hotel and looking at a bright red Dodge Charger parked in the 'Rental' slot. Dana hit the appropriate button on the key and the trunk '*clicked*' open. It was already more than half-filled by the gear Flame had received from Bremby.

"He's got a lot of stuff." Karin stared into the trunk as Dana pushed her bag into a gap.

"Not enough." The German girl jumped as Flame appeared out of the darkness. "Mapache is bound to have a lot of gunmen around him."

"Where were you?" Karin watched as the tall SEAL carefully stowed a rifle and combat vest in the remaining trunk space. "And why the rifle?"

"I was keeping an eye on you." He slammed the lid shut, made sure it was secure. "If Monasterio thought that it was to his advantage to shut you up..." He shrugged. "Well, it would have been a very bad—and very final—decision for him to make."

"You were protecting me!" Karin jumped forward and wrapped Flame in a full-body hug. "That is so nice!"

Dana, watching from one side, shook her head and smiled at the surprised and bemused look on Flame's face. "Tick tock!" She called out. "We're wasting time."

"We can explore this later," Flame disengaged from the German girl's embrace. "When we have more time." He kissed her nose. He pushed her into the back seat, waited while Dana got in and booted up her laptop, then shut the door and moved around to the driver's seat. "Right now, we've got a truck to catch." He slid the seat all the way back, turned the key, and burned rubber as he left the hotel driveway and headed for Highway 40.

***

Nearly two hours ahead of them, as Mapache's truck passed Saltillo, the boss's cell phone rang. "*Si.*" He spat out—then sneered as he recognized the voice at the other end. "What could you possibly do to help me?" He almost hung up but something the other man said made him stop. "How many of them?" He nodded slowly. "What kind of car did they rent?" Another nod. "Very good, we will be ready." A cruel smile creased his face. "And this time, you will be properly rewarded." He touched the off button.

"What was that all about?" Sautero was his most trusted associate—trusted enough to be allowed to drive the truck.

"There is a German reporter-bitch on our tail," Mapache spat the words out. "The original hospital administrator was her uncle and she wants answers." Mapache looked at his henchman. "Let us make sure that we give them to her, eh Sautero?"

"I will make sure of it, *jefe*."

"Good," Mapache settled back in his seat. "Wake me when we reach Chihuahua—I know a nice place to have breakfast there."

"Won't that give this reporter time to catch up?"

"Perhaps," Mapache closed his eyes. "It would be good to meet this woman." The smile returned to his face. "We might have some fun…"

Seconds later, he was sound asleep.

***

"You were right, Flame." Dana looked up from her laptop. "The captain sold us out, he called Mapache to warn him that we were on his trail."

"How did you know…" Karin was leaning on the back of Flame's seat. "Oh," she nodded. "The bug you left in the captain's office…"

"He figures telling Mapache about us will buy him immunity." Flame shook his head. "I think he's dreaming. Blanco will insist that there be no backtrail on this one—the captain had better get someone else to start his car every time he uses it."

"And taste his food," Karin shook her head angrily. "Bastard."

"He did us a favor." Dana was tapping away at her console. "I was able to use his call to find out Mapache's cell number," she leaned forward. "I can trace his location as his phone pings the closest cell phone tower."

"Where is he right now?"

"West of us," Dana leaned closer. "Moving…"

"He's in the truck with the Cobalt-60." Flame nodded. "Maybe we'll be able to intercept, stop him from reaching his destination." He pushed down on the gas, watched the speedometer inch up toward 50 KPH.

Chapter 28

A stern chase is a long chase, Flame knew that quite well. Now he was thinking about what he would do if he actually caught up with his quarry. *I can't get into a shootout while Karin and Dana are with me.* He knew that Dana had done a fine job in the Statue of Liberty. He also knew that her hands had still been shaking two days later. *Even so,* he thought. *She kept her cool in Monterrey,* he glanced at her as she worked her computer. *But I can't expect her to watch my back in a real shootout.*

Karin was a bigger issue. The German girl had a lot of courage—and even more nerve. *She'd insist on fighting alongside me,* he knew. *And she'd probably get herself killed in the process.* He shook his head. *I've gotta find a better way...*

Moments later, by pure chance, he had it.

"Mapache's on the phone again," Dana had used NSA software to monitor the gang chief's calls. "This time he's talking to someone with a very deep voice and an odd accent." She glanced at Flame. "I'll bet it's Blanco!"

"What are they talking about?"

"It seems that Mapache had planned to stop for breakfast somewhere just outside Chihuahua," she smiled. "Breakfast with Karin and me as a side dish."

"Dumb." Flame spat the word out. "They're making assumptions with no data."

"They are Mexican thugs," Karin shook her head. "What do you expect?"

"Blanco is no mere thug." Dana had gone through his dossier back in New York. "He's a smart guy—well trained and thoughtful." She grinned. "And he has forbidden Mapache stopping for any reason."

"How's our Mexican thug taking that?"

"Not well," Dana listened for a moment. "Not well at all." She held up a hand for silence. "That's interesting," she turned to Flame. "Blanco says the operation has to go off tomorrow—says he won't be able to guarantee his border guard beyond then."

Karin leaned forward. "What does that mean?"

"It means he's bribed a border guard to let him through." Flame answered.

"Bribery is a way of life down here," Dana put in. "Especially among police and public officials."

"Like Monasterio and that new hospital administrator— Dr. whatever his name was."

"Calvera." Dana nodded. "Yes, like them." She turned toward Flame. "What do we do?"

"We stay on their trail." Flame set his teeth. "And try to break up their plot before they get to the border."

"And if we fail?"

"We can't afford to fail." He pressed down on the gas, watched the speedometer display inch upwards. 50...51...52...

***

"Hey!" Karin yelled from the back seat—she'd pulled her own laptop from its bag and was doing some prep work for the article she planned to write once she finally got home. "Do you know how far it is to Ensenada?"

"About fifteen hundred miles, I think." Dana had the exact distance logged into her system somewhere but didn't think the other girl really cared about accuracy. "Why?"

"It's going to take us what, twenty-two, twenty-three hours to make the drive?" She leaned forward, looked from Flame to Dana. "Why didn't we fly?"

"No way to take my gear," Flame piped in. "No bribe is going to get anyone connected to an airline to take *that* stuff aboard!"

"Besides," Dana turned toward Karin. "There was nothing available that would have gotten us there in less than thirty-six hours." She shrugged. "I looked."

"Okay, so we have to drive." Karin nodded toward Flame. "Does that mean *he* has to be behind the wheel?"

"What do you mean?"

"I mean, is it smart to have him drive for a full day and then get into his commando suit and take on God knows how many bad guys?" She looked at Dana. "Does that sound smart to you?"

"She's right." Dana nodded and glanced at the dashboard. "We're going to need gas soon—when we stop to get it, you get into the back seat so you can get some sleep, Karin and I will drive the rest of the way."

"I'm okay," Flame waved off the suggestion. "Really—I don't need that much sleep."

"Flame," Dana leaned toward him. "You've got to let us do this—it's the only way we can contribute." She raised an eyebrow. "It's not as if you're going to let me go with you into Blanco's hideout, is it?"

"Of course not," Flame shook his head. "You don't have the training or…"

"I know how to drive a car," Dana kept her voice soft and sure. "Let me do that much."

"Okay," Flame realized that she was right—she was his partner and it was her right to demand a piece of the operation. "When I get gas…"

The Charger was a thirsty machine. They stopped for gas less than an hour later and, after filling the tank, Flame took Karin's spot in the back seat. It wasn't long enough for his six foot four frame to stretch out, but he had long since learned how to curl into any space available.

He was asleep before Dana rolled the Charger back onto the highway.

The dream started almost instantaneously.

***

Damn. Flame looked around at the darkness of the now far-too-familiar room with the even more familiar door in front of him and to his right. *Why do I always end up here?* He pulled down his night vision goggles and switched them on.

The world turned green and yellow.

Okay, he looked around. *Who's going to visit tonight…*

"Hey, babe!"

Flame whirled to find Mo a few feet behind him, smiling broadly.

"Had to get two girls to take my place, eh?"

"Mo, I..."

"Hey." She stood up, her naked body glowing in the night vision system. "I know the blonde one is your new partner. The other though..." Mo smiled. "She can't wait to jump your bones again!"

The redhead moved closer, reaching out a hand and running it down Flame's cheek. "Almost clean shaven," she laughed. "Much better than that day in Bagram."

"Why do I keep dreaming about you and Re-Pete and Manny?" Flame reached out, put a longing hand on the girl's shoulder. "Why can't I just sleep through the night?"

"I don't know why you keep dreaming about us, babe," she shrugged, the movement doing interesting things to her breasts. "You've got to answer that yourself." She tapped the scar on his forehead. "You know that it's all coming from in there."

"Besides," she took a step closer and planted a gentle kiss on Flame's mouth. "Do you really want to lose me forever?"

"I..." Flame reached out, tried to embrace the girl before him.

"You have a job to do," she slipped away, took a long step toward the door into darkness. "Maybe when you've finished..."

"Mo, please!"

"Later, babe." She smiled at him. "I'm always here." She took another step, opened the door, turned to step through...

And paused.

"Manny says to remember everything Chilli taught you about declination." She shrugged. "Whatever that means."

She smiled one more time—and stepped through the door.

Flame snapped awake—to find himself still in the Charger, still speeding through the Mexican countryside.

***

"Dream again?" Dana was looking down on him from the front seat.

"Not so bad this time." Flame clambered around until he was sitting upright. "What time is it?" He looked outside. "Where are we?"

"It's nearly five p.m. and we're about sixty miles from Ensenada." She held up a hand. "Mapache got there nearly an hour ago—I've got a good fix on his location."

"Good."

"Karin can really drive," Dana smiled. "Way better than me."

"Autobahn teaches you a lot." She took a quick look back at Flame. "Hungry?"

"Yeah," he nodded, suddenly aware of the empty feeling in his middle. "Got something?"

"We picked up some food when we last stopped for gas." Dana handed him a large foil-wrapped package. "The two of us assumed you'd want something."

Flame began to unwrap the parcel. "What is it?"

"It's supposed to be a beef and cheese burrito." Dana shrugged. "At least that's what the grandmother running the snack bar said it was."

"Tastes like chicken," Flame muttered around a mouthful. "Which, in my case, could mean almost anything."

"I have a beer for you as well," Dana held it up. "Dos Equis do?"

"Fine," Flame took another bite. "Anything new from the target?"

"He made a call to Blanco just before he arrived—he was told to go directly to the barn—I took a fix on where it was."

"Good," he gulped down the rest of the food. "Now pull up a Google Earth image and find me a way to get in without being seen."

"Already done," she keyed up the image, showed him the path she had traced through it. "It's about a mile in from this secondary road."

"Looks perfect." He stretched. "Now if Sabine Schmitz up there can just get us where we're going…"

"You know racing?" Karin glanced back at him. "Formula One?"

"Like *Top Gear*," Flame grinned. "Chilli and I are both fans."

"Automobile porn," Karin snorted and slowed down as Dana gestured to a side road. "You should watch the real thing."

"Maybe you'll introduce me to the sport." Flame stretched and finished his beer. "*After* this is all over."

"It is a promise!" Karin made another turn—this time onto a dirt road. "And one you had better come back to keep!"

***

Ten minutes later, Flame was suiting up. First came his Dragon Skin body armor, then a combat harness with extra ammo, grenades and his fighting knife. His Browning 9mm went into a cross-draw holster and a sawed-off Mossberg 500 8 Shot complete with an Insight Tactical Light slung over his shoulder. Finally, he hung a modified AR-15 from a Giles sling across his chest.

"Should be dark by the time I get there," he took the cased night vision goggles Bremby had sent and hung them over his shoulder. "Nice to have these."

"Be careful." Dana kept her face calm but Flame could see that her hands were shaking again. "Don't make me come after you."

"Monitor my radio," Flame tapped the earbug to make sure it was live. "And be ready to bug out if this goes shitside up."

"Formula One." Karin gave him a quick kiss on the cheek. "Remember your promise."

"Wouldn't miss it," he settled his gear and headed for the tree line. "See you both soon."

The girls watched as he moved into the woods—and disappeared from sight.

***

Flame took his time approaching Blanco's farm. He knew that the attack was planned for sometime tomorrow which meant (he hoped) that he had all night tonight to do whatever had to be done.

I wish I had someone to cover my ass, he thought as he moved along. *I feel kind of naked.*

He shook the thought away and concentrated on moving through the light underbrush as quietly as possible, finally emerging, just before sundown, on a little rise that overlooked what had to be the farm he'd come looking for.

Nice, he thought. *Cattle, horses.* He looked at the large ranch-style house set to one side. *All the comforts.* He brought his rifle up, peered through the Bushnell's AR 1-4x24mm sight that Bremby had mounted. *No movement,* he swept the reticle over the area. *No sign of anyone at all.* He turned the rifle toward the barn. *They must all be in there.* He sighed. *No way to tell how many there are...*

He settled in to wait for full darkness, double-tapping his earbud to let Dana know that he had reached the target area.

***

"He's there," Dana nodded at Karin as the two huddled in the car, eyes on the laptop. "He'll wait until it's dark to do anything else."

"And there's no way we can help him?"

"We'd just get in the way." Dana put a hand on the other girl's shoulder. "Don't worry—this is what he does, what he's been trained to do. He'll be all right."

"I hope you are right." Karin picked up a bottle of water and twisted off the cap…

***

A mile away, Flame drained one of the water bottles he had brought along. It never hurt to keep hydrated, he knew, especially when it was nearly time to kick off a mission.

He eyed the sun, which was almost below the horizon. *No street lights anywhere around here,* he looked around the farm. *No apparent lighting down there either,* he nodded. *Gonna be really dark in about twenty minutes.* He checked his weapons and pulled out the night vision goggles. *And SEALs own the night.*

He smiled and settled the goggles in place.

***

Inside the barn, Mapache's men had almost finished transferring the Cobalt-60 they had just hauled across the country into the larger casing holding the quantity they had acquired earlier.

It was a dangerous process, and one the men took great care with.

"Are they done yet?" Matias Blanco stood far to one side, supervising from afar. "We must be ready to leave by first light!"

"They are almost done," Mapache made a dismissive gesture. "All will be ready."

"And you are sure that you covered your tracks in Monterrey?"

"The hospital administrator is the only one who truly knew what we were doing." Mapache grinned. "He can tell no one—at least not in *this* world."

"What about the police captain?"

"He was helpful in telling us about the German reporter—I do not think he will talk to anyone."

"What of the German reporter?"

"She seems to be gone." Mapache said. "She left the hotel in Monterrey a few hours after we did and hasn't been seen since." He shrugged. "Perhaps she returned to the United States." He smiled. "If she brings her story to the State Department I am sure they will do everything in their power to help her, is that not so?"

Blanco barked a laugh, then turned as one of the men working behind him called out. "What is it, Grigorio?"

"The last of the material is in place, *jefe*." The man wiped sweat from his brow. "The truck is ready to go."

"That is good." Blanco smiled. "We will leave just after midnight and cross the border early, before things get too crowded."

"Indeed," Mapache leaned forward. "Now, as to our pay…"

"Of course." Blanco clapped the bigger man on the back. "Let me return to the house and I will get all that you have been promised." He smiled. "Just give me a moment…"

As he turned toward the door, the lights suddenly cut off.

***

Flame clicked on the night vision goggles and slipped through the barn door, scanning the floor before him for targets. He soon found there were ten… *No, eleven*—men in the room. Two had already pulled weapons from shoulder or belt holsters.

He would handle them first.

He let his reticle settle on the closer of the two—the one with what appeared to be a MAC-10. His finger touched the trigger, slowly squeezed…

CH-CLACK! The silencer swallowed most of the sound leaving only the metal-on-metal noise of the slide moving back as the round left the barrel then forward as it seated a new round in the chamber. Flame watched his target fall to the ground as he changed positions and searched for the other gunman. *There!* He raised the rifle, let the reticle touch the man's head and…

CH-CLACK! The second gunman fell. The others were in near-panic now, scrambling around the barn floor looking for cover of some kind.

Flame picked out a third man, put a round into his knee. *That should confuse the issue,* he thought as the man began to scream and beg for help.*Now if I could just find Blanco and Mapache…*

A pistol began to fire from his left rear—it wasn't aimed fire, just a panicked man shooting in hopes of hitting something—anything.

It didn't work.

CH-CLACK! The third gunman fell, his weapon clattering across the floor. Flame moved toward the hayloft—if he could get up high, he might be able to find his primary targets. He let his rifle fall to the end of its sling, and reached for the ladder…

Something struck him across the back, the impact driving him forward, into the ladder. *What the hell?* Flame whirled to one side, right hand clutching at the grip of the AR-15...

A giant of a man stood some five feet in front of him, holding what appeared to be a two-by-four, which he was swinging wildly from side to side. As Flame watched, the end of the wooden staff struck one of the milling men, knocking him to the floor.

I don't have time for this! Flame raised his rifle, centered it on the man's chest, and...

CH-CLACK! CH-CLACK! CH-CLACK! The man dropped to the floor, the wooden beam bouncing to one side. Flame returned to the ladder, climbed quietly upwards...

He was almost to the top when he heard the roar of a Diesel Engine. He rolled onto the loft, and brought the rifle to bear just as the truck the men had been working on accelerated forward and smashed through the barn *door.*

Shit! Flame tapped the earbud. "Dana! The truck just pulled out—dark colored, California plates. BB something. Mapache and Blanco are inside—see if you have any kind of fix on it." Flame ducked as bullets whizzed by—aimed at the sound of his voice. He rolled to his left, found one of the gunman, aimed...

CH-CLACK!

He moved again, found another target: *CH-CLACK!*

There were only three moving figures below. One was the man who Flame had wounded in the knee—he ignored that one. A second was hastening toward the broken door. Flame let his sights settle on that one, squeezed the trigger.

CH-CLACK!

The last man fell to his knees in the middle of the floor, begging the virgin for mercy.

She didn't answer.

CH-CLACK! Flame ejected the magazine in his rifle even though he knew it had twenty or so rounds left. He replaced it with a full magazine and slid down the ladder, taking a few minutes to search the barn. There was nobody left save the now-unconscious individual with the smashed knee. Flame left him where he lay and double-timed out of the place, anxious to get back to Dana and the Charger.

He had to catch the truck before it reached its target.

Chapter 29

"*¡Caray al diablo!*—God damn it to hell, who was that?" Mapache was at the wheel of the truck desperately steering between trees as he tried to get to the dirt track that he knew led back to the main road.

"That German bitch must have followed you." Blanco was equally desperate to get his seat belt buckled before his head went through the windshield. "Maybe she had someone with her."

"Who? SEAL Team Six?" Mapache manhandled the truck onto the dirt road. "Those were eight of my best men back there!"

"Forget them," Blanco had regained control of himself now that the tide had smoothed out. "We still have a job to do," he glanced at his companion. "I will double your fee if you get the truck to the target."

"Triple," Mapache gave him a cold stare.

"All right," Blanco nodded, a cold smile spreading across his lips. "It is only money."

The truck came to the end of the dirt track and turned onto a concrete roadway. Mapache pressed down on the gas pedal, anxious to get as far away from the devil in the barn as possible.

***

Flame was still cursing himself when he reached the car.

"I screwed the pooch," he tossed his rifle and shotgun into the trunk. "Big time," the combat vest followed. "I got so involved with the small fry," he slammed the lid shut. "That I let the big target get away."

"There was nothing you could have done." Dana had to run to keep up with Flame as he stalked toward the driver's seat. "You needed backup—and I wasn't there."

"Not your kind of fight," he jerked the driver-side door open, and motioned to Karin to get out. "You'd have gotten killed."

"Maybe," Dana grabbed Flame's arm, tried to turn him toward her—failed. "But I'm your partner—I should have been with you."

"That's stupid," Flame shook his head, glaring at Karin who had still not moved. "I'm the sharp end—you're the brains."

"Okay," Dana nodded. "I'm the brains—so listen to me—we can still catch up to those guys. We can still stop them."

"How?"

"Mapache and Blanco are in the truck. I have both their cell phones marked—I can follow them."

"Why didn't you say so?" Flame turned to look at her, eyebrow raised.

"I've been trying." She nodded to the other side of the car. "Now get into the passenger seat—I'll get in back and we'll go after that truck."

"But I want to drive!"

"Karin is better," Dana smiled. "Besides, you and I can plan our next move while she gets us where we're going—it's the smart thing to do."

"Smart," Flame shrugged. "Maybe…"

"So get in the car!" Karin slammed her door shut. "We are wasting time!"

***

"They're heading for San Diego," Dana announced a few minutes later. "And they've got quite a lead."

"Must've been a dirt road behind Blanco's ranch," Flame was staring at the little map on the laptop. "Left them off on a direct roadway."

"So what do we do?" Karin put in.

"We keep after them," Flame looked at Dana. "And you contact the admiral and tell him what's up. There're a lot of military personnel in and around San Diego—they've got to be warned."

"I already called the admiral," Dana told him. "Woke him up."

"And?"

"He'll put out an alert for the military bases—but he can't do much more without approval from higher authority."

"Terrific." Flame shook his head. "It's on us, then."

"What do we do?" Karin looked at their grim faces. "Where do we go?"

"You and Dana cross the border—stay on Blanco's trail."

"What about you?"

"I can't do any good without my gear," he nodded toward the trunk. "And there's no way I can sneak that past the border guards." He sighed. "You're going to have to drop me off somewhere along the way and let me sneak across."

"Is that a good idea?" Dana shook her head. "What if you get caught? By the time we got you free, this would be all over."

"I'm pretty good at infiltration techniques," he smiled and shrugged. "I don't think I'll have too much trouble."

"There is another way." Karin said, her face thoughtful. "A year or so ago I did a piece on immigration in the United States. I befriended several *coyotes* who told me any number of secrets." She nodded. "One told me of a tunnel from Mexico to the United States—and I know where that tunnel is located."

***

The tunnel was about ten minutes off the main road, dug into loose soil at the edge of the Parque de La Amistad. Someone had taken the time to cover it with some loose foliage but Flame spotted it almost at once.

"You're sure this is clear?" He began gearing up.

"It was last year."

"And big enough for me to fit through?"

"You might have to crouch down a little."

"Okay," he snapped his rifle into place, set the night sight goggles on his head. "Let's give it a go." He pulled the foliage off the tunnel's mouth, pulled aside the plywood that covered the entrance and took a long look inside.

"You two take the car and cross the border." Flame turned back to the girls. "Meet me on the other side." He smiled, sketched a salute—and dropped into the darkness.

Okay, he thought. *Not as bad as it could have been.* The entrance was about six feet below ground, the tunnel proper sloping downward in front of Flame. *It seems to be about five feet high.* He waited for the sound of the Charger pulling away. *Big enough for me to walk through if I crouch down.* He flicked on his night vision and started downward...

I wish I'd brought a flashlight, he thought about fifty yards in. *The footing is really uneven and the night vision is so two-dimensional...* He stubbed his toe on a thick piece of wood and swore to himself.

Whoever had built the tunnel had braced it with two-by-fours and scrap lumber. In some places, cross-beams had been nailed between the upright braces. They'd gotten covered with sand and gravel over time putting them just under the surface in a perfect position to trip the unwary traveler.

Can't worry about my toes now. Flame pushed on. *I have to get to the end of this as quickly as I can—before Blanco and Mapache reach their target.* He knew where most of the military bases in the San Diego area were—almost all were within a half-hour's drive of the border. He couldn't find the truck before it reached one of those bases—but he might be able to get to it before it detonated...

I've gotta be almost through, he thought a few minutes later. *I've come nearly a quarter mile—I can't believe they dug much further than that.* He sped up his steps, splitting his vision between the floor and the tunnel ahead.

And saw the door.

Shit! He stopped in his tracks. *Why is it always doors?* He took a deep breath, swallowing what to him was something akin to fear, and stepped forward, reaching out to touch the black surface.

Seems harmless enough. He gave it a gentle push—it opened to show utter darkness.

Flame stepped out—and was immediately bathed in bright light as the Charger barreled up the road toward him before sliding to a start less than six feet away.

"Get in!" Karin yelled, pushing the door open. "We know where Blanco is going!"

Flame tossed his pack into the back seat and jumped in. "What have you found out?"

Karin hit the gas, spun the car on its axis and headed back up the road already doing forty.

"Blanco made a call to arrange a pick up." Dana smiled. "The original plan hadn't called for him to be sitting in the bomb when it got to its target."

"Not surprising," Flame nodded. "The big shots never blow themselves up for Allah."

"Whatever, he told the person he spoke to—in Los Angeles, incidentally—to come get him near the San Onofre Power Station."

"Name sounds familiar." Flame pulled his shotgun out from behind his back, laid it on the floor of the car.

"It should," Dana showed him a picture on her laptop. "The politicians have been fighting about it for years. They're afraid to start the reactors—problems with the pumps."

"I remember now." Flame nodded slowly. "It's right off I-5—near Camp Pendleton, right?"

"That's the one."

"Hell, if they set off a dirty bomb and breached the containment domes…"

"Five or six million people live within fifty miles. Radioactive waste would wash into the Pacific—it'd be a huge mess."

"We've got to stop them," he said, and was thrown into the door as Karin sped onto the I-5 on-ramp.

"That's the plan." Dana tapped on the keyboard, and showed Flame the result. "Here's the truck," she pointed at a red dot. "Here we are."

"We're about ten miles behind."

"Not for long," Karin smiled and stepped on the gas.

The Charger sped north on the freeway.

***

They had just passed Oceanside when Karin saw the flashing lights appear behind her. "Trouble," she told the others. "I think we picked up a traffic cop."

"We don't have time to explain things," Dana thought for a second, then: "Give me the shotgun, Flame. Karin, pull over." She rolled down her window. "We'll do this as quickly as we can…"

The lights belonged to a CHP—a California Highway Patrolman on a motorcycle. He pulled up behind the Charger and strode forward, ticket book in hand. "Do you know how fast…"

"Don't move." Dana showed him the shotgun. "This isn't what it appears but we don't have time to explain now." She nodded. "Flame."

The redhead was already out of the car and behind the patrolman. He took the man's gun and handcuffs before leading him to the side of the road. There was a chain-link fence about twenty feet beyond the edge of the highway. Flame handcuffed the cop to one of the support poles. "Someone will find you soon enough." He removed the man's helmet and radio, placed them a few feet to the side. "Keys in the bike?"

The patrolman glared at him.

"If not, I'll be back to get them." Flame turned and jogged back to the car. "Give me the LAW rocket from the pack," he told Dana. "Looks like a cardboard tube."

"I know what a LAW rocket looks like!" Dana pulled the item in question out of Flame's pack. "What else do you need?"

"Keep the shotgun." He hadn't taken his vest off so now he just slung the rocket launcher over his shoulder. "I'll take the rifle."

"What do you have in mind?"

"I'm going to see if I can get in front of the truck." Flame clipped the rifle onto its combat sling. "If I do, I'll blow the engine with the rocket. The shock should take out Blanco and Mapache without detonating the bomb."

"And if it doesn't?"

"That's why I'm taking the rifle." He grinned. "Make sure the admiral knows what's going on."

"I will."

"See you at the back end," he ran back to the motorcycle, checked the controls, and roared off, lights blinking blue and white.

"Follow him," Dana said to Karin. "We're his only back-up."

"Getting to be a habit, is it not?"

The Charger accelerated into traffic, the rear wheels spraying loose gravel over the cursing policeman.

***

It had been a long time since Flame last drove a motorcycle—but the old skills came back very quickly. *This one is a bit more powerful than the last bike I drove*, which had been a cheap Honda back in Pensacola. *Let's see just how fast I can go...*

He hit the accelerator and crouched down over the handlebars. He had a truck to find.

***

Mapache grunted as they passed Oceanside. "We are almost there."

"Good," Blanco stretched. "We'll pull into the Freeway just before we reach the nuclear plant—some of my men will meet us there and handle the rest of the operation."

"I wish them luck," Mapache looked into his rearview mirror. "Looks like a highway cop coming up behind us."

"Don't pull over," Blanco shook his head. "If he tries to cut us off, just run him down."

"It will be a pleasure," Mapache grinned, eyes on the oncoming lights.

***

Flame saw what he thought was the right truck just ahead. *I'll have to be sure*, he thought, and accelerated, drawing up alongside long enough to get a look inside.

He saw the grinning visage of Mapache—who cut the wheel and tried to run him off the road.

They're playing for keeps! Flame avoided the attempt by accelerating past the truck. *But so am I.* He did some rapid calculations and pressed the accelerator, speeding forward until he was about a mile and a half ahead of his quarry, then he hit the brakes hard, slewing the bike sideways until he was across the truck's path, in line with its left tire.

By then it was a mile away.

He unslung the M272 and popped it open, pulling the tube to full length.

A half mile.

He set the sights directly between the truck's headlights.

Five hundred feet.

And pressed the trigger.

The LAW rocket flashed out of the tube, the fins clicking into place moments after ignition. Flame watched as the rocket flew straight and true.

Right through the front grate of the truck.

As designed, the front of the rocket's nose section was crushed causing a micro-second electric current to be generated. That detonated the warhead.

Flame had aimed the rocket at a slight angle so that when it went off, the copper liner, turned into a directional particle jet, flashed through the driver's side of the truck cutting a two-foot wide hole through the cab and, incidentally, Mapache's chest— before passing through the left-side door and dissipating in the air.

I hope their bomb is well-designed, Flame thought as he watched the nose of the truck dig into the ground, causing the vehicle to cartwheel—toward him!

Crap! He tried to restart the motorcycle, but it was too late, the truck fell less than four feet away, bits and pieces of the motor and cab cascading down the road all around him.

Flame ducked down as far as he could, using the motorcycle as a shield against the smaller pieces.

It did no good as a large section of the cab's roof smashed down on top of him.

Flame had a split-second to think that he should have figured the declination better before metal rained down on top of him, stunning him for a moment.

Then intense pain ran up his leg.

It's the door. He looked down at the driver side door assembly, which had landed on top of his ankle. *The damn door!* A piece of the door's metal casing had sliced into his leg, pinning him to the road.

He tried to push himself free—and realized that he wasn't alone. *There's someone alive in that truck!* He groaned as he made another attempt to get free. *If they have a detonator...*

The movement became a man—a short, fleshy man who showed white against the night. He was looking for something in the remains of the cab...

It's Blanco. Flame tried again to free himself—unsuccessfully. *He's searching for the detonator!* Flame reached for his rifle, pulled it up to his shoulder—and realized it was useless, the barrel hopelessly bent. *I can't let him set the bomb off here! There are houses all around the road!* Flame turned onto his stomach, desperately trying to pull himself free of the debris. He yanked hard, using all his strength...

Something tore and he felt blood ran down his leg. *Can't worry about that,* he told himself as he clawed at the asphalt road surface again, used all his strength.

His leg came free.

Finally! He pushed himself upright, turned toward the remains of the truck, reaching for his holstered pistol...

Too late.

Blanco was standing on top of the truck, a triumphant smile on his face, the detonator raised over his head. He started to pull the trigger...

Boom! Boom! Boom!

Blanco staggered as he was hit in the chest, flesh and bone disappearing with the impact. Already dead, he half-turned to see where the bullets had come from, the detonator dropping out of suddenly nerveless fingers...

And collapsed into a heap on the road alongside the ruined truck.

Flame sagged in relief as he saw Dana appear, his shotgun over her shoulder, and pick up the detonator. "We've got to stop doing things this way, Flame." She smiled. "You're supposed to be the sharp end!"

He laughed as the first helicopter appeared on the horizon.

Chapter 30

Flame's leg only needed a few stitches and a temporary brace. He was up and around by the time the CBR Team from Camp Pendleton finished examining the bomb in the truck. It had been shrouded with over one hundred-fifty grams of Cobalt-60—enough to contaminate everything within fifty or sixty miles.

They unloaded it with great care, taking it, ironically enough, to the San Onofre containment building until it could be disposed of.

The admiral arrived an hour after dawn, summoning Flame and Dana to the office he'd commandeered in the Marine compound.

"You two did a tremendous job," he smiled. "Better than the idiots running the show deserve."

"Thanks," Dana shrugged. "You did ask us to look into it."

"I did indeed," he leaned back in his borrowed chair. "And I will see that you're properly compensated for your work."

"Ms. Hachtel helped too, sir." Flame had seen to it that the German reporter had been given a room so she could rest and freshen up. "Without her," he shrugged. "We might have been too late."

"I'll have to think about what we can do for her." The admiral ran his eyes over Flame. "Aside from the obvious." He ignored the hint of a blush that crossed the ex-SEAL's face.

"As for you two," he pulled a file out of his briefcase. "I have an offer for you." He looked from Dana's eager gaze to Flame's confused one. "The terror threat has gotten to the point that the government is hard pressed to properly combat it." He leaned forward. "Too many plots are being hatched and assembled in countries friendly to the US—where our agents can do little or nothing."

"CIA," Dana began.

"Is muzzled thanks to Edward Snowden." The admiral made a throwing-away gesture. "We need assets that are not part of any government apparatus."

"So you can 'disavow' them."

"Just so," the admiral grinned. "Now, the CIA director and I have come up with an idea—we call it ESS."

"Another acronym?"

"It's Washington," the admiral shrugged. "It's what we do." He tapped the file. "ESS stands for External Security Services." He smiled. "It means we can establish a string of independent contractors who we can call on in certain situations."

"Funding?" Dana had seen some hints of this while still in the CIA—and she hoped she had divined where the admiral was going.

"Black funds." He shrugged. "Money is not an issue."
He leaned forward. "You'd have to be ready to drop whatever
you're doing and take a mission from us with no questions."

"We can do that." Flame smiled. "Hell, we
just *did* that!"

"We'll need more people." Dana touched Flame's hand.
"I can't back him up forever."

"We'll pay for that—although we'll want to clear
whoever you decide to hire." The admiral passed the file
forward. "This is the new 'Official Secrets' Document—if
you're prepared to become part of ESS, you'll both have to
sign."

"What do you think, Flame?"

"Sign it," the redhead shrugged. "We'd do the job
anyway—at least this way we get paid." He smiled. "And hurry
it up—I have a date to see a Formula One race."

"The next one isn't until Saturday."

"I know that," his smile widened. "I think I can find a
way to pass the time." He looked at Dana. "And if I fall asleep, I
don't think I'll worry too much about my dreams.

About
Doug Murray

Doug Murray has been:

A soldier in the Viet Nam War;
A Bank Vice President;
A teacher of history and English;

And, throughout all these other things, a writer of, as his friend Peter David says, _stuff_. He is the creator/writer of THE'NAM, the critically acclaimed comic book series about that unpopular war. He has also written hundreds of other graphic stories about characters as dis-similar as The Punisher and Roger Rabbit, and Conan and Uncle Scrooge.

He has also written hundreds of film reviews and articles about films and filming as well as several novels and short stories (including a children's story which is still utilized as part of the reading curriculum in several states).

"It's been a pleasure to work on this SEAL TEAM SIX spinoff/sequel. Too often men separated from the military end up ignored and underutilized by a government that really doesn't understand them. It's good to show that such men can be a positive part of the fight against those who would harm Americans.

Sources

For the most part, I have utilized the same sources as Chuck Dixon for information about SEAL team operations. I have also leaned on his books for help and inspiration. Information about NSA and CIA Tech and tactics come from various sources including the leaks and revelations of Edward Snowden.

U.S. Navy SEALs by Samuel M. Katz
1993 Concord Publications

SEAL Sniper Training Program
1992 Paladin Press

US Navy SEALs
by Robert Glenat
1992 Windrfow & Greene